DARK OBSESSIONS

USA TODAY BESTSELLING AUTHOR

LEXI C. FOSS

Dark Obsessions

Editing by: Outthink Editing, LLC

Proofreading by: Katie Schmahl & Jean Bachen

Cover Design: Nousanti Art

Title Page Design: Maria Spada

Interior Chapter Art: Jessica Allain

Interior Image of Ciprian: Elle (@mageonduty on Instagram)

Interior Image of Vivi: JV Arts

Published by: Ninja Newt Publishing, LLC

Digital Edition

ISBN: 978-1-68530-414-0

Print Edition

ISBN: 978-1-68530-415-7

AI Disclaimer: This book does not contain any elements of AI content. All art was designed by real artists, and all of the words were written by the author.

To Emanuel, for showing us around Transylvania and being amazing with Baby Foss. Romania is a beautiful country; I can't wait to visit again.

To my friends and family who ventured around Romania with me, don't read this. Ciprian has a tail. It does things. I don't need you reading about those things. Okay? Okay.

And, to everyone else, Ciprian has a talented tail and a tantalizing tongue. He also has a magnificent wingspan and other impressive attributes. Enjoy. ;)

DARK OBSESSIONS

When the Strigoi King says, "Kneel, pet..."
And his fated mate replies, "Make me."

"Monsters Are Real."
That's the title of my master's thesis.
It's also why I'm in Romania.
Hunting. Scouring. *Searching.*

Because I know he's here.
Ciprian Negru, King of the Strigoi.
He's the heart of my research.
My damnable obsession.
My downfall.

I assumed he had no idea a measly human like me even existed.
I should have known better.
Because he's been waiting for me.
Lurking in the shadows.
Stalking my every move while I stalked him.
And I just waltzed right into his trap...

You're mine now, Viviana Dalca.
A pretty little toy to use.
To break.
To claim.

So be a good pet and kneel for your king, sweet girl.
Because I'm about to show you how dark this mutual obsession goes…

Author's Note: *Dark Obsessions* is a standalone dark romance with monster vibes. If you enjoy possessive antiheroes who lack morals and adore depravity yet handle their heroine with the utmost care, then you've come to the right place…

ABOUT DARK OBSESSIONS

Dark Obsessions is a standalone monster romance in the Monsters of Darkness shared world. This series showcases various standalone stories by different authors. None of the stories overlap, and there are no shared characters. Therefore, they can be read in any order.

Please note that this is a darker series that features monsters who don't think like humans. They take what they want, with or without consent.

That said, some of the books are darker than others. *Dark Obsessions* is on the "lighter" side of the darkness because Vivi is just as obsessed with Ciprian as he is with her.

But he will test her limits.

Safe words will be involved.

And there will be dubious-consent content with a hint of nonconsent toward the beginning. Ciprian is a Strigoi King. A monster of the darkness. Not a shining white knight. So don't expect him to think like a human. He's incapable of that kind of compassion.

But he is possessive. Enjoys hearing his female say yes

more than no. And will do whatever it takes to win her over in the end.

If you're looking for heavier noncon, I recommend reading some of the other books in the series. However, if you're okay with dubious consent (leaning heavier on the consent since Vivi is overall willing to play), then *Dark Obsessions* is the right book for you.

Happy reading!

Below are some themes you may find in *Dark Obsessions*…

✓ MF Romance

✓ Psychotic Obsession (both ways)

✓ Bratty submissive / Impatient Dominant

✓ Dubious Consent

✓ Somnophilia (light content, more "petting while she's asleep" sort of thing)

✓ No Other Woman or Other Man Drama (No Cheating)

✓ Pregnancy/Breeding

✓ Primal Energy

✓ Possessive Over The Top Alpha Male

✓ Touch Her and Die Vibes

✓ Nesting, Purring, Growling & a Lot of Tail Play

Enjoy! <3

PROLOGUE
CIPRIAN

Negru Castle, Carpathian Mountains

"I don't understand what you see in this realm," Marius mutters as he kicks a loose rock along the stone floor. "Mortals are so… *fragile*."

"Their blood sustains my beast." It's an emotionless answer, one I don't wish to elaborate upon. Particularly as my best friend and confidant is very aware as to *why* I've chosen to reside within this realm.

"That's a bullshit reason, Cip." Marius only calls me *Cip* when he's trying to piss me off. It sounds like "*sip*," and I fucking despise the witless nickname. "The immortals back home sate our thirst just fine, and you know it."

I grunt. *Immortals* is a false term. The humanlike beings of our home realm are only *immortal* because their genetics respond favorably to Strigoi venom. Essentially, they provide blood to us as necessary sustenance, and our bites stop them from aging.

It's created a boring existence, one that lacks a proper

hunt. Which I've explained to Marius on countless occasions.

I refuse to be like my predecessors, all of whom relied on the trials to help them find suitable matches. I much prefer the notion of choosing someone for myself, then offering my intended mate to the Strigoi for approval.

It should save me some of the heartache my father experienced. In theory, anyway.

Regardless, Marius knows all of this.

Yet he continues to riddle me with these incessant inquiries.

"If you're tired of leading the kingdom in my absence, just say so, *Mars*," I state flatly, using the nickname I've given him in response to *Cip*.

"You have a harem of seven very willing blood slaves," he deadpans. "Trust me, I am not bored by that."

I roll my eyes. "You created that harem after I left." I had merely one or two blood whores I used back home, and only for biting.

That was also partly why I left.

Nothing there roused my interest.

Alas, no one here seems to be doing it for me either.

Most Strigoi indulge in sex while feasting on their prey. Not me, though. I've never desired more than a few sips from the vein.

Which makes it fucking impossible to create a Strigoi heir or heiress—something that is my duty to provide as the Strigoi King.

Not even others of my kind have intrigued me enough to fuck.

What I need is a toy I want to use for more than feeding.

The mortals of this world at least provide me with a challenge, particularly as monsters lurk in the shadows here, not out in the open. That means I have to be clever about my hunts, taking prey only at night, and wiping their minds before they wake.

A few have piqued my interest.

But when it came time to do more than eat, I was suddenly bored again.

I need a mate.

My beast seems convinced that she's destined to come from this land of humans. I just haven't found her yet.

Sighing, I glance up at the moon—the pale color I still haven't learned to like. I miss the blood-red moons of my homeland. The crisp breezes that never still. The waters that run crimson, not blue.

This world of humans varies in temperature and climate, boasts unique horticulture throughout the globe, and creates a vast space of uniqueness everywhere I go.

This region of Transylvania is my preferred location, though. The forestry here is reminiscent of my world. Except there, it's black and silver in color, not green.

"Why is your wrist buzzing?" Marius demands as my watch begins to vibrate.

I glance down at the warning scrolling across the screen. "It's an alarm."

I don't elaborate on what that means, instead leaving the balcony and heading inside through the double doors of my study. Had I been on any of the other outdoor patios or terraces, I would have teleported. But, in this case, walking takes roughly the same amount of time.

"I gathered it's an alarm," my best friend says as he follows me inside. "An alarm for what?"

"Search algorithms," I murmur, taking a seat at my desk. My monitors automatically turn on, my movement triggering a sequence of electronic processes to spur to life. A scanner confirms my identity, thus allowing me to log in to every program without so much as touching my computer mouse.

Then the cause of the alarms plays across my screen.

Marius asks me a clarification question about algorithms, but I ignore him, not in the mood to explain the highly elaborate security protocol that I've crafted for monitoring potential threats in this world.

Technology isn't his strength. Nor was it mine until recently. However, I've had a lot of time to study this new era of digital information and social networking.

"Hmm," I hum, intrigued by the search details appearing before me.

Someone has been looking into the Negru estate. That's not abnormal. The castle is infamous for being off-limits. But I pay the requisite government officials a handsome sum to allow me my privacy. And those who push a little too hard are simply glamoured into compliance.

Although, whoever is researching this topic—the history of deed transfers that I falsified throughout the centuries—appears to be noticing patterns that few others have picked up on. Mostly because it seems this individual has been studying the signatures, as well as other historical occurrences.

Purchases of furniture.

Contractor bills.

Things most humans shouldn't be able to find because I signed many of those forms under other names. Or didn't sign anything at all and simply used glamour to achieve results.

Who are you? I wonder, surprised as more search history appears on my screen. *How long have you been researching my estate?*

"What is all of this?" Marius asks, leaning against my

desk as he stares at the three monitors with a furrowed brow. "It looks like dozens of web browsers."

"Because it is dozens of web browsers." I glance at him. "I'm surprised you even know that term."

He grunts. "I've been visiting you enough lately to learn the phrase."

"Yes, and why do you keep visiting me?"

"Because I'm bored."

"Then your persistent question as to why I'm in this world instead of our home one should answer itself, Mars."

His silver-blond eyebrows lift. "The Strigoi King makes jokes now?"

"Never," I growl. Then return my focus to the screen just as an illustration of me from the sixteenth century pops up. My lips part. "*Where* did you find that?" I marvel out loud, clicking on the item to locate the source of it.

A library scanned it from an ancient text in Dublin, Ireland.

Trinity College.

Hmm.

I follow the source material and use my fancy tools to alter the image file with something else. I also make a note to visit Trinity College personally to steal the textbook.

Of course, it's too late for whoever has already downloaded this piece of damning evidence.

Because there's a print icon on the screen.

Which means she or he has already created a paper copy.

Fuck.

"Who are you?" I ground out, needing to know the identity of this nuisance so I can personally handle the issue.

"Who are you talking to?" Marius asks.

I ignore him, instead striking several keys on my keyboard as I attempt to hunt out my new prey.

When a name appears, I pause.

Because it's a rather pretty name.

Viviana Dalca.

Her details begin to list themselves before me.

Twenty-two years old.

Graduate student at The Ohio State University.

Doctoral candidate pursuing higher education degree with focus on classics studies, specifically folklore.

My jaw clenches.

More words appear, the evidence making me sigh with dread.

Because she's clearly obsessed with vampire lore.

Probably some young girl who grew up reading tales inspired by truths she'll never actually believe.

A dreamer. A writer. *A future nuisance.*

I've met her type before. Glamoured my share of them throughout the years. It seems this female will be no different.

Though, admirably, she's come closer to the truth than any of the others. Because that illustration she pulled of me is one I didn't even know existed.

It shows my wings and tail—two traits rarely associated with vampires in this realm—as well as my pointy ears.

Hmm.

I drum my fingers across the table.

Maybe I can play with this female. Turn her into a toy. Or at least introduce her to the nightmare of my existence.

Let's find out who you are, Viviana, I think, clicking on the file that will take me to her social media pages. *You've seen me, so now it's time for me to see you…*

CHAPTER ONE

VIVI

BRAȘOV, ROMANIA

Three Years Later…

Vampires are real, and I am going to prove it.

I stare at the screen, reading the first line of my thesis, and drum my fingers against the table.

As far as opening statements go, this one captures the essence of what will eventually become an eighty-thousand-word doctoral dissertation.

I'm about to begin documenting my hellacious travel day—which actually equates to more than a day's worth of hours, thanks to my prolonged layover in Paris—when my phone dings.

Did you find your vampire yet? Gaby, my best friend, asks in her message.

I snort. *I landed in Bucharest not even five hours ago, G. Baggage claim took forever, as did the rental car place—so many rules, by the way—and it was a complicated-three hour drive here after all that. I'm exhausted.*

Three little dots appear and disappear as Gaby contemplates her reply.

Vampires don't sleep is what she finally sends back to me.

I wait for more.

But in classic Gaby style, she doesn't say anything else. However, the implication is clear. *I'm a night owl, G. Not a vampire.*

Uh-huh, she types back. *Says the vampire hunter.*

You basically just called me a slayer, G. That implies I want to kill my quarry, which I don't. That last part is added out of superstition.

I'm certain the object of my research has no idea I'm here.

I mean, why would he? I'm just a human.

But on the off chance he's aware of me—and also reading these messages—I feel it's necessary for him to know that I have no desire to harm him.

I still think you should try to fuck him, Gaby responds, as crass as ever. *The books I've read make it sound like an otherworldly experience. Pun intended.*

My lips twitch. *Biting is supposed to be euphoric.*

That's what I'm saying, she replies. *I just hope he doesn't glitter in the sun, you know?*

I shake my head. *You're ridiculous.*

I'm curious, she counters. *I'm also not the one who flew all the way to fucking Romania to hunt a mythical creature. But I digress.*

Sighing, I type back, *The whole point of this adventure is to prove that myths are founded on reality.*

Yeah, yeah. I can practically picture her waving her black-polished fingers at me in dismissal, her usual gothic ensemble part of her charm. She's probably wearing tight leggings and a ripped shirt—both black to match her nails, of course.

Meanwhile, I'm in jeans and a sweater, my messy brown hair pulled up in a bun, and a pair of glasses perched on my nose.

We make quite the pair when out in public.

She approaches life with an "I don't give a fuck what you think about me" attitude, while I hide behind my books.

Somehow, it works for us.

You don't have to sell me on this adventure, V, Gaby writes to me. *I'm not on the scholarship committee.*

I roll my eyes, her comment referring to a discussion we had months ago when I first started planning this study-abroad experience.

"And how do your scholarship providers feel about you using academic funds for a vampire-hunting vacay?" she asked me after I excitedly told her about my plans to finally visit Transylvania.

"It's for research, G," I informed her, my voice flat.

"Research," she repeated. "I mean, I guess fucking can be considered research."

"Fucking?" I echoed, confused. "I'm going alone… and I don't plan on hooking up with anyone while I'm there."

"What about the vampire?" she drawled. "I mean, you will fuck him if you find him, right?"

My best friend and her monster-romance obsession.

I've read several of her book recommendations, though. And, well, I get it. However, I would never admit that to her out loud.

Nor have I ever confided in her about my dreams.

I simply keep telling her that this project is for academic purposes, not personal ones.

She doesn't believe me.

That's fine. I don't believe my motivations most days, either.

Hey, it's stupid early here, so I'm going back to bed. I just wanted to make sure you haven't been eaten by a vampire yet.

I huff a laugh and shake my head again. *Go back to reading, G.* Because we both know she's not actually sleeping. She was probably up all night with a book.

Let me know when you find your vampire. I need to know if his dick glitters.

I send her a sun emoji, then set my phone down to stare at my computer screen. It's… way too late to try to recount my journey here. I'll just do it in the morning.

After I get some much-needed sleep.

And food, I think, my stomach rumbling as I put my laptop away.

I can't remember the last time I ate. I don't even really know what time it is, either. Just that it's late here. Although, Brașov appeared to be very much awake when I parked my car on a nearby street.

Grabbing my bag and room key, I put on my shoes and leave to explore the main plaza outside my hotel. There are numerous places to eat, along with a myriad of people wandering about.

But I pause to just… admire the view.

It's nothing like Columbus, Ohio—where I've lived my entire life. It's flat there. Busy in a different way than this, especially on campus. And just… freer. Maybe it's the nearby mountainscape, or the fresh air, or the fact that I don't know a single person here. However, I feel liberated. Like I'm entering a new world.

I stare up at the city name built into the mountainside, my lips curling into a smile. The letters are lit up for everyone to see, creating a stunning sight that I merely admire for a few moments before shifting focus to my food options.

Most of the places are still open, and a quick search on my phone says they don't close for another hour or so. Seems the area caters to late-night meals. Or maybe ten is normal here. I'm not sure. That wasn't part of my research preparations, but I make a mental note to look it up later.

Entering a place only a few yards from my hotel, I request a table and then peruse the menu. It's all foreign. Not surprising, considering where I am.

Fortunately, my phone helps me translate, and I eventually settle on some sort of meat dish. "Good choice," says a male voice to my left, shortly after the waiter leaves.

I blink at the tall man, wondering if he's talking to me.

Given that his dark eyes are locked on mine, I assume he is, so I reply, "Er, thank you."

He smiles, allowing me a glimpse of matching dimples on each pale cheek. "Want some suggestions for dessert?" he asks, his accented voice warm and a little too alluring.

I can only imagine what Gaby would be saying right now. She'd probably be cheering me on, demanding I mix business with pleasure, and blah, blah, blah.

But I'm not her. She's confident. Beautiful. Goes after what she wants.

Meanwhile, I date fellow graduate students, none of whom have ever held my interest for long.

However, this stranger smiling down at me doesn't know any of that.

And he's still waiting for a reply.

"Sure," I force out, wanting to appease my inner Gaby-inspired voice.

The handsome male slips into the chair across from me and drags his fingers through his silver-blond hair, the ends of which touch his muscular shoulders.

His pale features are more Nordic in nature, making me wonder if he's a lonely traveler just seeking out some company while venturing around Romania… or if he's a local who enjoys picking up solo women.

Regardless, I'm curious.

Even though I shouldn't be. I should be eating and sleeping. Maybe showering, too.

Yet I decide to indulge this unexpected occurrence and arch a brow. "Will you be joining me for dessert?"

"Depends on what you order," he murmurs, his intense blue eyes dancing over my features. "What's your favorite fruit?"

I shrug. "I like anything sweet."

"And how do you feel about cream?" he asks, making me wonder if that's supposed to be an innuendo for something else.

"Depends on how it's served," I reply, still channeling my inner Gaby.

"Hmm," he hums, glancing away from me for a moment before focusing on me once more. "Do you like cake or pie?"

"Again, I like anything sweet," I tell him. "I'm really not picky."

He nods. "Then any dessert I suggest will suit you."

"Most likely, yes," I admit.

He folds his arms on the tabletop, drawing my gaze to his muscular form. He's wearing a knitted sweater, the fabric not tight, yet revealing his strength at the same time.

"What brings you to Romania?" he inquires, changing the topic. "Business or pleasure?"

"Both, I guess." I fidget a little in my chair, suddenly feeling a bit exposed. I don't like talking about myself. Dessert preferences are one thing. My studies are… quite another. "I'm here for research."

"Oh?" He leans forward, intrigue written across his features. "What are you researching?"

"Mythology." It's a vague response, but explaining my doctoral thesis would take hours.

"Mythology," he repeats, like he's tasting the word. "From medieval times?"

"Something like that," I say, not wanting to elaborate. "Why are you here?"

He smiles, his dimples appearing again. "I'm a tour guide."

My brows lift. "A tour guide?" I suppose that explains his perfect English. I mean, there's an accent, but he's clearly fluent.

He dips his chin. "Guilty as charged." He scrutinizes me for a moment. "Do you have any tours planned?"

I stare at him, understanding finally breaking through my mind.

This guy isn't hitting on me or flirting with me. He's trying to woo me into hiring him for a tour. I almost laugh out loud at the realization, but I'm too exhausted to put forth the effort.

Instead, I just shake my head and tell him the truth. "The castle I want to visit doesn't have a tour available."

He leans forward even more, his interest palpable. "Which castle do you want to visit?"

I don't bother lying to him. "Negru Castle."

His blue eyes widen. "You really have done your research, haven't you?" He glances around, then lowers his voice as he says, "What if I told you I could take you there?"

My lips twitch. "Then I would know you're trying to make me pay for something you can't deliver on."

He leans back a bit, evaluating me once more. "What if I promised to take you and accepted payment after?"

My eyebrow inches upward. "Then I might accuse you of trying to kidnap me."

He laughs, the sound warm and infectious. "I'm not much into kidnapping these days. Guiding tourists into castles is more fun." He shrugs. "Besides, it's been a while since I last visited Negru Castle. I'm almost tempted to offer a tour for free."

I still. "You've been to Negru Castle?"

"Of course," he replies.

I narrow my eyes. "You're lying."

"I'm not."

"Prove it," I dare him.

Because I've been researching Negru Castle for the last three years and I know for a fact that the general public isn't allowed on the property, let alone inside.

It's a private residence up in the Carpathian Mountains, owned by a family that no one has seen in centuries. Yet the paperwork continues to get mysteriously passed down to each new generation.

But there are no pictures or identifying images.

Just signed documents.

All of which appear to be penned by the same hand. It's illegible. And the printed name is redacted.

On. Every. Page.

Whoever owns that property does not want to be found.

Which is exactly why I'm here.

Because I suspect he's the mythical beast I've been hunting. The one illustrated in ancient texts. A creature with wings. Red eyes. Pointed ears. And a tail.

"This is from my last visit," the stranger tells me, holding up his phone and distracting me from my thoughts.

I blink at the image before me.

It's a recognizable staircase, one spiraling up through a modern living area to a third-floor landing. Paintings line the walls, ones known to be owned by the Negru estate.

I look at the man in front of me and then the man in the image.

They're definitely the same person.

But…

"Is this photoshopped?" I ask.

He chuckles, turning the phone back toward him as he starts to scroll. Rather than answer me with words, he simply turns the screen in my direction again as a video begins to play. His voice carries through the speaker, but the language isn't one I understand.

It's not Romanian, as I've spent the last few years studying it for research purposes.

Instead, it sounds harsher. More Slavic in nature. Yet the words are unrecognizable.

However, the scenery is familiar.

It's him walking outside Negru Castle, the beautiful fields of flowers and trees nestled into the mountains showcased in abundance as he strolls down a long pathway toward an enormous estate. The Neo-Renaissance architecture is undeniable, as are the stained-glass windows.

My heart skips a beat as the one depicting a woman lounging in a bed of bloody flowers comes into view. It's famous. Or, perhaps, *infamous*. Because it's said to be a tribute to vampire brides, specifically the ones of a well-known literary vampire.

I shiver, the piece speaking to me like it always does. I've dreamt of being that woman. Which is crazy. Yet sensual in a way I can't deny.

The door of the castle opens to reveal a male standing just inside, his body large and imposing in the shadows.

My lips part. *Is that…?*

The video ends, and I suddenly feel like weeping. I was so close. Only, not close at all.

Because I'm sitting at a table in Brașov.

With a stranger holding a phone.

A stranger who has actually been to Negru Castle.

Because some of those video panoramas included him smiling at the screen like a selfie before refocusing on the immense scenery.

"Believe me now?" he asks, arching a silver-blond brow.

"Who are you?" I whisper, unable to keep the awe out of my voice.

"Marius Scaevola," he replies, holding out his hand. "And you are?"

Completely captivated, I think, reaching out to place my palm against his. Fortunately, I don't utter that aloud. Instead, I say, "Vivi Dalca." I stare at him, our hands joined in an awkward shake. "How soon can you take me to Negru Castle?"

"Shouldn't you ask me about costs first?"

I shake my head. "You take me there and you can name your price."

"A dangerous prospect."

"The heart of my research is a dangerous obsession," I tell him. *Or a dark obsession, anyway*. "Tell me when we can leave, and I'll be ready."

CHAPTER TWO
CIPRIAN

"I CAN'T BELIEVE THAT WORKED," I mutter as Marius joins me in the shadows outside Viviana's hotel.

"I told you it would," he drawls, taking the phone from his pocket. "She liked the video."

My eyes threaten to roll, but I'm too focused on Viviana's window to allow my gaze to move. "I want that video destroyed."

"After I escort your little researcher to your doorstep, I'll happily toss this into an open fire," he tells me, holding up the phone for me to see one more time before slipping it back into the pocket of his gray slacks. "She might want to watch it again in the car."

"Fine." I don't say anything else about it, just watch as the light flickers off in her room. "You're not charging her for the tour."

"No, I intend to charge you instead," he says.

I'm again tempted to look at him but can't shift my focus away from my quarry. Her scent is like a fucking drug. I inhaled it shortly after she arrived in Brașov, the blood-orange citrus swimming in the wind and taunting my inner beast.

Gods, she smells better than I could ever have imagined. It makes me wonder why I waited for her to come to me.

Fuck, I should have gone to her.

Dragged her out of her dorm apartment.

Taken her against a wall.

Made her fucking mine three very long years ago.

It feels like forever ago since that fortuitous night when my systems alerted me to her existence, sending me on a beautiful chase through the interwebs as I sought to learn everything about Viviana Dalca.

The moment her photo appeared to me that first time, I froze, shocked by the innocence staring back at me.

This little human is stalking me? I wondered, intrigued.

After several minutes of reviewing her research history, it became clear that the curious little creature had been studying me for *years*. But it wasn't until she started looking at the property deeds—specifically my signature—that alarm bells went off.

A flaw in my programming, clearly, as I should have been alerted to her presence two or three years before my system went off.

Because it seems my sweet little stalker has harbored a dark obsession with vampires for a very long time.

Well, I'm not a vampire, pet, I think. *I'm the fucking King of Strigoi kind.*

And she just entered my trap.

My world.

My nest.

I'm going to make her regret ever embarking on this research journey.

Make her realize how dangerous her fixation truly is.

Make her wish she never discovered my existence.

Her tears will taste divine. They'll be a decadent appetizer before I enjoy her blood as my main course. *And maybe her body for dessert…*

"You're growling," Marius informs me.

"And?" I press, aware of the rumble that's ignited in my chest. It's taking serious restraint not to wrap myself in shadows and teleport into my intended pet's room. Introduce her to my wings. My tail. *My cock.*

But I want her in the confines of my estate before I play with her.

In a place where no one will hear her screams.

"The sound is reverberating through the square, Ciprian."

"So maybe a storm's coming," I reply, finally looking at my oldest friend and confidant. "Humans always explain away a supernatural's presence. I've told you this a thousand times."

"Yes, I'm aware their minds can't fully embrace the truth of our existence. But what's that saying? Seeing is knowing? Understanding? Accepting?" He shakes his head, sending his silver-blond hair cascading like a waterfall around his head. "I really don't fancy having to glamour anyone who happens to *see* you right now."

"Then eat the mortal instead," I say, slipping my hands into the pockets of my dress pants and returning my gaze to Viviana's window. "They're food, Marius."

I don't usually kill my prey. But if he doesn't want to go through the trouble, he can just finish the job or take the human back to our home world. I don't really care so long as it doesn't become a regular occurrence.

That happened a few centuries ago—not with Marius but with a former rival that I killed for creating an inconvenience for me in this world. I'm still fighting the rumors that whole incident created.

Which, interestingly, is about to bring the little mouse upstairs to my doorstep.

My insides burn at the prospect, my mouth salivating for a taste of her.

Fucking glorious citrus…

She's a craving I'm longing to satisfy.

Since the moment I first traced the strands of research history to her, I've been *obsessed*. Her thick brown hair will look amazing in my fist. And those innocent, dark eyes will cry so beautifully while I shove my cock down her throat.

Gods, I can't wait.

I have centuries of lust built up in my veins, all of it waiting to be released… *on her*.

She'll beg me to stop. Then beg me for more. Because I'm going to become her addiction. Her air. *Her master.*

I've never taken a toy before, always preferring just to feed, glamour, and release.

Humans are too fragile to suit my needs.

But Viviana Dalca is going to learn how to take me. Please me. *Kneel for me.*

She wanted to find a vampire. Well, she's going to have to accept a Strigoi King instead. *Me.*

"You're growling again," Marius mutters.

"Not all of us are gifted with the ability to hide our monstrous traits," I return.

"Gifted or stunted?" he asks, aware that I often favor the latter term when referring to Marius's peculiar talents.

"Tonight?" I glance at him. "Tonight, I consider it a gift, as it allowed you to engage in conversation with my pet in a human space. I suppose I'll feel similarly tomorrow as well. Ask me again in a week, though, and perhaps my opinion will have changed yet again."

He grunts. "Your *inability* to mask our enviable—not monstrous—traits is why I continue to question your preference for this world."

"I'm not engaging in meaningless conversation with you again," I tell him.

"And since when is she your *pet*?" he demands, ignoring my comment entirely.

I repay the favor by not acknowledging his inquiry and wrapping myself up in shadows instead.

Then I teleport up to the room I've been watching for far too long. The light went out only a few minutes ago, so my prey might still be awake. That's fine. Unlike Marius, I don't mind a little glamour.

Especially when it comes to my intended pet.

But one glance at the bed tells me glamouring won't be necessary. Because my prey is already asleep, her pretty gaze hidden beneath closed eyelids dusted with thick, dark lashes.

Hmm. I move forward, my steps silent.

The sleeping female has no idea a predator lurks in her room. She's too innocent to sense me. Too mortal. Too *delicate.*

I take in her petite frame, barely concealed beneath the thin sheet. *Are you wearing anything underneath it?* I wonder, reaching down to gently tug the fabric away from her shoulders.

Twin straps of cream-colored silk meet my gaze, the fabric alluring against her light-colored skin. What's even more alluring, though, is how the tank top clings to her curves as I reveal more of her.

Seems my little mouse enjoys sensual nightwear, I think, admiring the outline of her nipples beneath the satiny texture. I can almost determine the color of those stiffening peaks, but not quite. *Mmm, soon, though…*

My tail twitches behind me, eager to play.

A little introduction won't hurt, I decide, allowing the triangle tip to flicker up to her bed—to the leg tucked beneath the sheets.

My eyes slide back up to her face, watching for any sign that my slight touches are disturbing her sleep. But all she does is part her plump lips like an enticing invitation.

This female appeared much more studious online, reminding me a bit of a young librarian. Scholarly. Intensely focused. *Soft.*

She still possesses all the traits from the photos and videos I've seen of her, yet she's even more tempting in person. Maybe because of her scent. Or perhaps it's her luscious mouth. It looks so sensual now, that invitation still lingering…

The tip of my tail travels up along her side, memorizing the subtle curve of her hips to her tiny waist, skimming the fleshy mound of her tit before reaching the bare skin of her shoulder.

A hum of electricity shoots through me, stealing my breath and causing my nostrils to flare.

Fucking divine, I think, captivated by my prey.

It takes every ounce of control that I possess not to lean down, lift her into my arms, and teleport us both back to Negru Castle.

I want her to come to me. *Willingly*. It makes her the hunter in this scenario and me the prey.

Which is a unique turn of events.

Perhaps that's what has roused my sleeping beast.

You sought me out, sweet pet, I think, my tail moving up the slender column of her throat. *And now you're going to experience the consequences of your obsession.* I allow the triangle tip to trace her lower lip, the sensation of it going straight to my hardening cock.

My body responds to Viviana in ways I've only ever dreamt about, making me pant with *need*.

"Gods, princess," I breathe, my voice too low for her to hear. "I'm going to enjoy destroying you." My tail dips between her parted lips to tease her tongue before slipping out to draw a wet path down to her neck. I pause against her pulse, my fangs tingling in my mouth. "Your blood sings to me."

The confession leaves me in a whisper, my heart skipping a beat.

No other human has ever made me salivate like this before.

All I want to do is lean down and *bite*.

Fuck, I want to do a lot more than that. However, I pull my tail back, refusing to give in to the temptation tonight. I only came up here to see her. To taste her scent on my tongue.

And to mark her as mine.

Which I've done with a few strokes from my tail.

Any other monsters in the area will know to leave this female alone until I'm finished with her. And that includes my best friend, the forever flirt.

Marius will have her in his clutches tomorrow as he drives her through the Carpathian Mountains. Yet it'll be *my* scent filling the car, not hers.

My lips curl, pleased.

Viviana Dalca is my female. My human. *My pet.*

Welcome to my world, princess. I can't wait to make you crawl…

Against my better judgment, I bend to brush my lips against hers.

My first kiss…

Fuck.

I instantly want to kiss this woman again.

Which is why I teleport out of her room before I lose

control of my inner beast. He's hungry. Dying for a bite. Begging me to *fuck*.

I've always sated my savage side with blood, nothing else.

But Viviana has awakened something inside me, something that won't be satiated until I've claimed every inch of her.

Her existence has enchanted me, creating this dark obsession.

Now she'll be the one to help me satisfy these urges. Even if it means breaking her fragile form in the process.

Poor little pet, I think, materializing in the shadows once more outside her building. *I wish I could go easy on you, Viviana. But it's just not in my nature. So sleep well, princess. You're going to need all the rest you can get…*

CHAPTER THREE

VIVI

CARPATHIAN MOUNTAINS

For a tour guide, Mărius isn't all that chatty. He's said a few things about our surroundings, commenting on the vegetation and wildlife—focusing mostly on the black bear population—while primarily concentrating on the road.

I would be a little more concerned if I weren't tracking our progress on my phone. But he's heading right for Negru Castle.

By my calculations, we'll be there within the next thirty minutes.

My stomach knots at the prospect. Or maybe it's in knots from my weird dreams last night.

I woke up shortly after falling asleep, an unexpected scent in my nose. *Lavender with a splash of vanilla.* Very specific. And utterly unlike everything else in my hotel room—a fact I learned this morning when I tried to find the source of the fragrance. I already knew my own products weren't the cause, but I thought maybe one of the complimentary soaps might be the culprit.

Nope.

Nothing matched the crisp lavender or subtle vanilla.

However, the aroma chased me into my dreams, creating a chaotic fantasy involving the heart of my research—*Count Negru.*

That's not his real name. But that's what I call him, the mythical creature that isn't so mythical.

My vampire.

What if he visited me last night? I think, my heart skipping a beat.

It's a fool's desire. A ridiculous fancy driven by my compulsion to hunt him. However, I allowed that fantasy to play through my mind all night, dreaming about my obsession and pretending that scent belonged to him. That he found me. Touched me. *Did other things to me…*

My thighs clench, my mind whirring with dangerous thoughts. I shouldn't be this obsessed with a mythical creature. This hungry for his touch. His—

Marius clears his throat. "Right, so, Negru Castle is about fifteen kilometers from here. When we arrive, the gate should be open for us, thus allowing us to drive all the way up to the front entrance. There are no tours today. Or, well, ever, really. So it should be fairly easy and quiet."

I nod.

Then I frown.

Because his words… his comments… *There are no tours today. Or, well, ever, really.*

I… I know that part. I'm aware that Negru Castle is a private estate that doesn't allow visitors.

Yet somehow I failed to question how Marius—a complete stranger to me—has access to the grounds.

Why didn't it occur to me to ask?

Oh, right. Because he showed me that video and I jumped at the opportunity to hire him.

My lips twist to the side. *I may have made an impulsive decision…*

Which should make me nervous. Or perhaps prompt me to send an SOS to Gaby.

But I didn't come all the way here to hide or approach this with caution.

I came here to find a vampire.

To prove that monsters exist.

That means meeting one.

I glance at my driver.

Or two… I narrow my gaze.

Marius *is* extremely handsome. Maybe even unworldly so. The way the sun streams into the car makes his blond hair almost resemble white gold. His jawline is chiseled in that model-perfect kind of way. His eyes are hidden beneath a pair of shades, but I saw how deep blue they were last night.

Although, he doesn't have fangs when he smiles.

And he's out during the day.

Is he a familiar? I wonder, aware of the lore that vampires keep human lackeys. *Is that how he booked this tour? Have I been… set up?*

"You mentioned being a tour guide," I say slowly. "But where are you from again?"

"Nowhere near here," he murmurs.

That's not a helpful answer. In fact, it feels intentionally vague. "If you're not from anywhere nearby, then how have you managed to secure a tour with a private estate?"

He glances sideways at me, his lips curling up on one side. "Does it matter?"

Not really, I nearly admit. Instead, I ask a question I think I may already know the answer to. "Do you know someone inside Negru Castle?"

His focus returns to the road. "I know many individuals, Ms. Dalca."

Individuals, not *people*. That… feels specific. And yet

intentionally vague again, too. "Do you know Count Negru?"

"Count Negru?" he repeats, his brow furrowing. "Is that his rumored name?"

"His?" I echo.

Marius's jaw clenches. "Are we playing a word game, Ms. Dalca?"

"I don't know, Mr. Scaevola. Are we?"

He says nothing for a beat, his hand tightening on the steering wheel. "You're not going to jump out of my car, right?"

I look out the window at the surrounding forest. "That wouldn't end well for me."

"Nor me," he mutters. "So please don't try it."

"Worried about the mess?" I wonder aloud, studying him again.

"Something like that." He's no longer smiling, his humor seeming to have died as our conversation turned real.

"You're not a tour guide, are you?" It's more of a rhetorical question at this point. I should be terrified. Thinking of an escape plan. Texting Gaby. *Something*.

But I started ignoring my self-preservation instincts when I began obsessing over Count Negru.

"Do you want a real answer, or a playful one, Ms. Dalca?" he asks, once again avoiding my inquiry. But I don't need an answer to the tour guide query. I know he's something—or *someone*—other.

"A real answer to a legitimate question," I counter. "Does *he* know we're coming? The Lord of Negru Castle? Or whatever his name is these days?"

"The one called Count Negru?"

"That's my nickname for him," I admit. "Because none of the records actually depict a first name. They're all variations of *lord* and *king* in other languages." That's something I determined early on in my research while pulling the property deeds. "He changes it when he transfers the estate to the next generation."

Marius smirks. But it's not the carefree, teasing grin from earlier. This is a bit more sinister. "You speak of these things without any fear."

"Because I've been researching his existence for years. I know he exists. And I know what he is."

"And what's that?"

"A vampire," I reply without hesitation.

"Hmm," he hums. "An interesting assertion."

"A correct one."

"Is it?" he counters, glancing at me again before refocusing on the road. "What else do you know, little researcher?"

"I know you're avoiding my questions," I inform him flatly.

"Indeed," he admits. "Because they're not mine to answer."

"Meaning he knows we're coming." Not a question, but a statement.

"Meaning I should stop talking," he replies. "Just do me a favor, Ms. Dalca, and remain seated. I don't want to have to chase you."

I don't understand his statement until we come to a crossroads that requires him to stop.

Rather than even consider the door, I fold my arms and stare him down. "I'm not afraid of him."

"I believe you." The car resumes speed before he adds, "Which has me questioning your mental state. Humans don't believe in supernatural occurrences. Your kind is always rewriting what you see. So why are you different?"

"My kind?" I focus on that part of his statement

instead of the rest of it. "If you're not human, then what are you?"

He merely shrugs. "Maybe I'm a vampire, too."

"Are you?" I ask, my heart skipping a beat in my chest.

"No," he replies. "Not a vampire."

And my heart sinks. "Oh."

"You sound disappointed."

"Because I am," I admit, twisting forward again to stare out the window before us.

"You're that eager to meet your doom?" he muses. I can feel his eyes on me, but I don't bother looking at him again. Instead, I focus on the trees framing the street—a street that appears to be narrowing ahead. "You realize humans are food for vampires. Yes?"

I don't reply.

Because yes, of course I realize that.

I just don't care.

I can't explain this obsession or why it seems to matter more than my own life, but it does.

If Count Negru wants to eat me… I don't think I'll be able to stop him. Heck, I might even *encourage* him.

"I never claimed to be sane," I mutter, the words ones I've said to Gaby countless times.

"That's fine," Marius replies, drawing my attention back to him. "Sanity is boring." His gaze meets mine briefly through his sunglasses before returning to the road. "At least I know why you're so calm. If you were of sound mind, you would be screaming right now."

There's not a whole lot for me to say to that, so I remain quiet.

"I'm thankful, though," he adds. "That you're being quiet, I mean. Not because you're saving my eardrums, but because screaming is an aphrodisiac. And you, my darling little researcher, are expressly off-limits."

His nose scrunches with the words, then his expression smooths out once more.

"Anyway, you requested a real answer to a legitimate question, so I'll oblige you with one. Yes, he knows we're coming." The car slows to a crawl as he approaches a gate.

The iron bars swing forward before we can come to a full stop, the grounds seeming to automatically open for us to enter.

"In fact, he's expecting you for dinner," Marius goes on. "I'm under strict instructions to take you on a brief tour before introducing you to your new quarters."

A fluttering sensation takes off in my chest. "My new quarters?"

Marius doesn't elaborate. Instead, he navigates us down the long drive—framed by an open courtyard blossoming with unique flowers and bordered by the forest beyond. It's magical, reminding me of another world, and that feeling I experienced last night in Brașov returns.

The one where I feel like I've left my reality and stepped into a storybook.

"You're definitely not a tour guide," I mutter, more to myself than to Marius. Though, the words are about him.

"I'm a tour guide today," he offers. "So, technically, not a lie."

I grunt. "Okay."

"I elaborated on some trivial facts on our way here," he points out. "And I'm supposed to provide you with a brief rundown of the castle grounds. That's very tour guide–like."

"You also claimed not to be into kidnapping these days, and yet…"

He smiles. "Kidnapping implies taking someone without their consent. You very willingly slipped into my car this morning, Ms. Dalca."

He slows the car again as we near the front of the castle where a fountain sits in the middle of a circular drive. Navigating around it, he parks us close to the entryway steps, then slides out from the driver's seat and rounds the front of his vehicle to pause outside my door.

Marius opens it, then waits for me to decide how I want to proceed.

"It's still technically kidnapping," I inform him as I unbuckle myself and join him outside. The crisp air carries a note of lavender that curls around me in an enticing caress, one that reminds me of last night. *My dreams…*

I swallow.

He was in my room, I realize. *Count Negru… was in my room.*

I'm certain of it. Not just a fantasy. Not just a thought. But a reality.

Because his scent is *everywhere* here. Or perhaps he just carried this aroma with him when he visited me at the hotel.

Regardless, he was there.

And now… now I'm *here.*

Outside Negru Castle.

About to be given a tour and shown to my *new quarters.*

"I never said I wanted to *stay* at the castle," I add, my words for Marius. "There's no need to prepare a room for me."

He smiles. "You don't really think he's going to let you leave, do you?" He leans down, his long silver-blond hair tickling his shoulders. "Tell me you didn't come all this way to find a vampire without considering the consequences of your desires."

I can't tell if he's toying with me or not. Part of me hopes this is a joke. But a larger, more insane part of me…

hopes this is real. That I've finally found the object of my obsession. That said object is planning to keep me.

And how fucked up is that?

I should not want to be kidnapped by a vampire. Or forced to stay in a castle.

Yet every part of me tingles at the prospect.

I've utterly lost my mind. That much is clear.

And I can't seem to bring myself to care.

"I guess you should take me on that tour, then," I tell him.

He straightens, surprise filtering through his features. "You're a fascinating creature, Ms. Dalca," Marius says softly. "Let's see how long you keep this unique confidence, hmm?"

CHAPTER FOUR
CIPRIAN
NEGRU CASTLE

MY PET IS HERE. The thought warms my blood, making me eager to find her, take her, and *taste* her.

However, I calm myself by merely enjoying her citrusy scent, the perfume wrapping around me in a welcoming invitation.

She's wandering through the main corridor with Marius, her brief tour of my estate coming to an end. He showed her the dining area—where I expect her to present herself at seven o'clock sharp—the main living rooms, the library, and the grand staircase, and he's now leading her through the residential quarters.

I wrap myself in the shadows, lurking at one end of the hall as she approaches the room I've designated as hers.

"How long will I be staying?" Viviana asks my best friend, her voice soft.

She's accepted this fate without a fight, something that intrigues me greatly. It makes me want to see how far I can push her before she breaks.

"Indefinitely, I imagine," Marius drawls, his answer making my lips twitch—something I'm glad he doesn't see because he would have about a dozen remarks to make in response to me *smiling*.

Not that my mouth fully curled upward or anything.

But that wouldn't matter to my second-in-command. Marius is *constantly* grinning. A trait I find absolutely ridiculous.

"Indefinitely?" my pet echoes, her cheeks taking on a delectable shade of red as she faces my best friend. "You realize people know where I am, right?"

"Do they?" he asks, his eyebrow inching upward. "Or do they just know you ventured to Romania alone to go hunt down a vampire?"

She narrows her eyes. "There are at least a dozen people who know I'm obsessed with Negru Castle."

Marius leans against the wall beside her future room, his arms crossing. "Is that meant to concern me? Because it doesn't." He reaches out to tuck a strand of her hair behind her ear, nearly causing me to materialize out of the shadows. "You really didn't consider the consequences of this obsession, did you?"

She merely stares up at him. "Considering the consequences and caring about them are two very different concepts, Mr. Scaevola." With that, she opens the door to her room.

Marius glances toward me—no doubt sensing my presence in the shadows—winks, and then follows her inside before closing the door.

My jaw clenches. He knows better than to touch my toy. But that doesn't mean I like him being alone in a room with her.

Of course, he just spent hours in the car with her, too. However, that was because I couldn't exactly drive her here.

I take a step forward, my hands fisting at my sides.

I could introduce her to her room. Show her the dress I left for her on the bed. Explain the clothes in her drawers.

Only, I tasked Marius with those items because I thought they were beneath me.

Now, I'm not so sure.

Now, I want to… remove him.

And take over.

It's her scent, I decide. *It's fucking drugging my senses.*

Before I can do something asinine, like storm into her room and throw Marius out the balcony window, I teleport to my office and pour myself a blood martini.

When I feel Marius join me several minutes later, I decide to make him one as well. Mostly to curb his appetite. *Viviana is my pet, and I will* not *be sharing her.*

"Your little researcher is strange for a human," he comments as I hand him the glass. "I expected more fear."

"She's been researching me for years. And she came here willingly, knowing what I am."

"Well, she thinks you're a vampire."

"To her standards, I am," I tell him. "But I'll correct her terminology tonight when I introduce her to my fangs."

"Pretty sure vampire lore involves fangs, too."

"Semantics," I mutter, taking a sip of my drink as I pull up the video feed from Viviana's room. She's currently standing beside the bed and running her fingers across the dark red dress I left for her there. "Did she agree to my dinner invitation?"

"I didn't phrase it as a choice."

"Good." Because it wasn't an offer but a demand. However… "I just want to know how she responded to it."

"With arousal," he growls, causing my eyebrows to lift.

"Arousal?"

"Yes." He takes two healthy gulps of his drink before

looking at me. "I'm rather certain your pet has been turned on all damn day, something I would have enjoyed more if she weren't also doused in your fragrant claim."

My lips almost betray my inner amusement. But with Marius's open scrutiny, I manage to keep my stoic expression. "That's interesting."

He just shakes his head and finishes his blood martini. "Am I free to leave now that I'm done being your errand boy?"

"Missing your harem?" I wonder aloud.

"Very much."

I nod. "I think I can handle it from here."

He sets the glass in the wet bar sink at the back of my office. "Enjoy your new toy, Ciprian. Maybe she'll be your ticket home." His silver wings appear as he heads for the mirror that leads to our realm. It's anchored into the wall and framed by mystical stones from the Strigoi world.

"Ticket home?" I ask, aware of what he's implying. "She's not a candidate, Marius." She's simply the first mortal I've been interested in tasting. It could be thousands of more years before I find someone I feel comfortable enough to bring home for the trials.

And I won't let the experience become a spectacle.

I am *not* my father.

"Then I hope you enjoy using her, *Your Highness*." He gives me a mock bow, then steps through the glass before I can comment.

Sometimes, my best friend is useful.

Sometimes, he's infuriating.

Today, he was both.

"Typical," I mutter, then return to my desk to watch the female walking across my monitors. She's left the dress on the bed and is now looking through the drawers of her dresser. Her eyes widen as she pulls out the translucent fabric waiting for her inside.

"What…?" she whispers, then holds it up to herself like she's trying to figure out how to wear it. "Yeah, no. I'm not wearing that."

I snort. "You'll absolutely be wearing that," I reply, aware that she can't hear me. But I'll inform her of the rules at dinner. "Or you can choose to walk around naked."

Either option works for me.

She opens more drawers, her lips pinching when all she finds are more lingerie sets.

Then she stomps over to the closet, which is filled with evening gowns and nothing else.

Well, there are shoes, too.

I wanted the option to dress up my toy, so I decided to provide a few different styles to see what type of dress looks best on her. I went with a blood-red gown for tonight, primarily because I fully intend to ruin it by feasting on her flesh.

Viviana walks back out of the closet with her pretty eyes narrowed at the bedroom door.

My lips twist upward for the second time today when she tries to open it and finds it locked.

"*Ugh*," she grinds out, the sound causing my grin to grow into a smile.

This show of irritation pleases me. I was beginning to worry that she might kneel for me willingly. But this means I'll have to work for her submission.

And that… that intrigues me.

I like the idea of forcing her to her knees and choking her with my cock.

Making her growl around me while I force her to take more.

Come down her pretty throat. *Drown her.* Then lay her flat against the table and feast between her thighs on blood and ecstasy.

Mmm. "I'm going to enjoy mastering you, princess."

I just hope she holds my interest longer than the rest. I've spent years pining after this female. It will be utterly depressing if my craving is sated just by tasting her blood.

Like all the others before her, I think.

Except there have never been obsessions quite like this.

I've stalked prey. Fed on them. Released them.

But those were passing fancies that lasted *minutes*, not *years*.

Either this is all a yearning crafted in my mind, or this is something more.

I'm not sure which outcome will be worse for her. Disappointing me or being forced to handle lifetimes of lust.

We'll find out soon.

Tonight.

At dinner…

CHAPTER FIVE
VIVI

I HAVE NO CELLULAR SERVICE.

Not surprising, given that I'm in the middle of nowhere in the Carpathian Mountains.

Though, I'm not sure what I would write to Gaby if I could. *Hi. It's me, your crazy friend. I went to Negru Castle with a stranger, and now I'm locked in a beautiful room overlooking a courtyard. The count wants to have dinner with me in five minutes. And he's making me wear a sexy red dress, too.*

Gaby would probably reply with something like, *Sounds like one of my favorite books, V. Let me know if he glitters…*

Or she would freak out and tell me to get the hell out of here.

The latter is probably what I should be feeling. Instead, I'm just staring at the door and waiting for Marius to unlock it from the other side.

I'm not afraid. I'm… I'm something else entirely. I'm a ball of nerves, the flutters in my belly overwhelmingly appropriate. This is it, the culmination of all my research.

Count Negru is real.

And I'm about to meet him.

My pulse races, probably for all the wrong reasons. He's a vampire. A monster. I… I shouldn't be *excited* to see him.

Yet I can't help the way I feel.

When a *click* sounds through the room, I hold my breath and wait.

But the door doesn't open.

Frowning, I stare at it, then try the handle and find it unlocked.

"Why are you…?" I trail off when I reveal an empty hallway beyond the threshold. "Umm." I peek out to look left and then right. "Okay…"

So the door auto-unlocks.

"Yeah, that's not creepy at all," I mutter to myself.

My heels—which not only fit me perfectly but also make me three inches taller—clack against the wood floor of the corridor as I leave the bedroom. I found them in a box beside the red dress on the bed, along with a note that read *Ms. Dalca, Dinner is at 7:00 p.m. Dress appropriately.*

I'm not sure how *appropriate* this clingy gown is, as it feels more like lingerie than a dress, but at least I'm not cold.

Negru Castle's exterior may boast an otherworldly and historic appeal, but the interior is definitely current with the times.

There are modern features throughout—such as motion-sensor lights and warm water that automatically turn on with a single wave of a hand—and thermostats to control the temperature in the bedroom and en-suite bathroom.

When Marius showed me the kitchen earlier, I noted all the advanced tech while wondering idly if vampires actually eat food.

There are no drafts anywhere that I've felt, not even in

the big open spaces like the grand staircase that I'm walking down now.

The massive front doors are latched shut, making me wonder if they're locked on the inside *and* the outside. But I don't bother trying to test the theory as I pass through the foyer. There's no point. I'm not running. I've been craving this day for years.

With my shoulders back, I head through the front living area—there are several others throughout, only two of which I actually saw on my brief tour with Marius—and into a space with a cocktail bar and lounge chairs.

"For an empty castle, there sure are a lot of places to socialize," I told Marius earlier.

He chuckled in response, then took me into the kitchen, which is where I go next.

It's huge, the size of which I would expect to find bordering a cafeteria, not a traditional dining hall. Though, I suppose the oversized room does have a table large enough for at least twenty chairs to sit around it.

Still, this all feels rather extravagant for a single vampire.

"Does anyone work in the castle?" I asked during my tour.

"Yes" was Marius's reply. He didn't elaborate. However, I've yet to see a single person other than him today. Probably because I've only actually been here for about three hours—it was a long drive—and I spent most of that time locked in a bedroom.

With drawers and drawers of lingerie, I think, shivering.

Count Negru must have had a former mistress. Maybe another vampire. Or a human. But that's the only explanation I have for the closet of formal gowns and the dresser of sexy nightwear.

The fact that it all seemed to be my size is… well, it has

to be a coincidence. There's no way he bought all of that in less than twenty-four hours. And I'm pretty sure some of those labels were in French, suggesting they would have been shipped in from France.

Count Negru couldn't have known that I existed until last night, and that's assuming Marius even told him about me at all.

Well, he had to have said *something* since I'm here.

Still, there's no way the count had time to purchase all of those items for me in such a short amount of time.

Unless meeting Marius wasn't a coincidence at all. That thought is one that's occurred to me several times today, ever since I realized that Marius wasn't really a tour guide. And that he might be a familiar or something else entirely.

There's only one way to determine the truth.

And that's by entering the dining room.

Taking a deep breath, I step through the threshold and find the table lit with candles. There are two place settings, one at the end and the other right beside it. There are also several food dishes situated nearby, all with serving utensils, but the lids are closed, making it impossible to know what's inside.

This might all be for show, something my nose seems to agree with since there are no lingering scents in the air.

Well, nothing other than the lavender and vanilla.

I inhale, loving that aroma and searching for the source. Because I know it's him. I can't explain how I know that. But it's just like when I first started researching Count Negru. I've always known what he is, and I've refused to believe otherwise.

"Hello, Viviana."

Goose bumps pebble along my arms.

That voice doesn't belong to Marius.

It's darker. Deeper. More cultured in nature. *A stronger accent.*

It's English… I think. Regal. *Crisp.*

The shadows of the room seem to move, the candles decorating the walls flickering in response.

I try to find the source of the movement, the source of the *voice*. But I can't see him. He's everywhere and nowhere at all, his scent stronger now and wrapping around me in a wave of eroticism. I… I feel like kneeling. Lowering my gaze to the floor. *Begging* him to reveal himself.

"Count Negru," I breathe, trying to be respectful and respond to his greeting. Because this is him. It has to be. Who else would be in this room, commanding such energy? Exuding this wicked of a presence?

"The title of *Count* is beneath me," he replies, the world seeming to shift as the shadows again taunt the surrounding light. "I'm a king, pet." The outline of wings becomes visible, causing my heart to flutter wildly in my chest. "The Strigoi King."

A Strigoi, I think, familiar with the term from Romanian folklore. It's come up several times throughout my research, the myths similar to the vampire legends I've studied. But never in reference to *him.*

He steps into the light, causing my lips to part. His muscular stature is encased in a pale suit that's clearly been tailored to fit him perfectly.

Because it's framed around his *wings.*

Enchanting bat-like wings.

Gray in color.

Just like the illustration…

Only, his jet-black hair is shorter now, the ends dancing around his pointed ears.

But the tail is exactly like it was depicted in that image. I know because that's the part of him I studied the most.

Something about it *captivates* me. And seeing it in person is no different.

It's a deeper red than the illustration, almost appearing black in color.

Or maybe it just appears that way because it's wrapped around his leg, creating an enticing contrast against his light-colored suit pants.

"This is the part where you kneel, Ms. Dalca," he tells me, drawing my gaze up to his square jaw and the beautiful full lips that just spoke.

However, his words have me focusing on his alluring gaze. So otherworldly. So *stunning*. Like obsidian stones glittering in the sun.

His almond-shaped eyes are mostly humanoid, just... decidedly *powerful*.

He lifts one black brow, the action reminding me that he told me to kneel.

I could. I *should*. I even wanted to moments ago.

However, I don't obey the request.

Because some part of me wants to challenge this male. An inane, ridiculous, rebellious part of me. A part of me that says, "Make me."

A bold choice, one I didn't expect to make. But deep down, it feels right.

That dark eyebrow of his inches even higher. "I will happily make you kneel, Ms. Dalca." The reply is smooth. Seductive, even.

And accompanied by movement as he strides toward me.

But it's not his legs that catch my attention so much as his tail.

The triangle tip touches my ankle, eliciting a gasp from me as it slides up my calf and along the back of my knee to my thigh. His palm grasps my nape in the next moment just as his tail wraps around my legs.

I yelp as my balance tilts.

Yet he doesn't send me to my knees.

He… he pulls me into him instead, his gaze capturing and holding mine in an intense embrace that forces me to stop breathing.

He's real.

I knew that already.

However, seeing him, being *here*, it's a dream come true. A fantasy come to life.

So many years of research. So much certainty. *So many nights wishing…*

Tears fill my eyes, the emotion overwhelming and suffocating.

His gaze narrows. "What is this?" he demands. "Tears, already? I've barely touched you, Ms. Dalca. If you're going to break before we even begin, then this is a most disappointing—"

"I'm not *breaking*," I interject. "I'm *relieved*."

He blinks. "Relieved?"

"Yes." I stare up at him, mesmerized by the perfection in his features.

He's a monster.

A *vampire*.

I know this.

I… I should be terrified.

Yet all I want to do is touch him. Assure myself that this is happening. That he's standing before me. *Fisting my hair…*

He studies me, his brow furrowing. "Marius was right about you being a fascinating creature."

I shiver.

I remember Marius calling me that last night in the restaurant.

Then suddenly I'm looking up at the Strigoi King from the floor.

My knees should hurt from hitting the ground. Yet they don't.

Maybe I've lost my ability to feel.

All I can focus on is his intense stare and the flicker of red that appears in his otherwise black irises. I feel hypnotized. Lost. *Utterly consumed.*

"This is how I expect to be greeted, Ms. Dalca. Preferably with your lips parted just like that so I can feed you my cock as I please."

His words send a jolt through me, one that seems to stir me from my delirious mental state. "*Excuse me*?" The words leave me even as a flurry of sensation warms my lower belly.

Because something about kneeling for him feels right.

And the idea of him feeding me his cock?

My thighs clench. Yeah, I like that a little too much.

Which is insane. Or maybe it's magic. *Am I enthralled?*

Of course I'm enthralled. I've been enthralled by the myth surrounding his existence for years.

Count Negru's grip tightens in my hair as the tip of his tail slips up my leg—*beneath my dress.*

My eyes widen, my body tensing.

Then I gasp when he strokes my *hip*.

"Cotton?" he asks, then tsks. "That is not what I expect you to wear. Satin, lace, or *nothing*. Understand?"

I blink. "What?"

He gives me a bored look. "It would be wise not to vex me with cluelessness, Ms. Dalca. We both know you heard me without issue. So be a good pet and remove that offensive material from between your thighs."

My jaw… *drops*.

I… I'm torn between being offended and doing exactly what he's requested. It's confusing. It's thrilling. *It's wrong.*

"I don't even know you," I manage to force out.

Of course, the words lack heat since they're not really true. I know everything about him. Rather, I've… I've researched him for a long time.

But I thought he was a vampire.

And I actually have no idea what to call him other than *Negru.* Maybe that's his first name. I'm not sure because he didn't really introduce himself. Just called himself a Strigoi King.

Then proceeded to start talking about kneeling and—

His grip in my hair tightens. "Human formalities don't exist here." His tail traces my underwear, the pointed tip making me shiver as it slides beneath the fabric. "This is *my* nest. My expectations. My kingdom. *My rules.*"

A gasp escapes me as his tail slices through the thin cotton strip, freeing it from one hip.

"You will obey," he goes on as that triangled end glides along my lower belly. "You will feed me. Pleasure me. Do whatever it is that *I* desire. Because I'm the king here. And you're my new pet."

Fire licks up my spine as the fabric loosens on the opposite side, his appendage having cut right through the fabric with a tiny flick.

I'm frozen.

Not with fear.

Not with uncertainty.

Just… just *frozen.* Because I have no idea how to respond to any of this.

I knew he would be dangerous. Cruel, even. It was a risk I was very willing to take. Heck, it was a risk I *desired.*

I've dreamt of him a thousand times. I thought the fantasies were simply inspired by Gaby's books. But maybe… maybe they were glimpses of the future. Of this *Strigoi King* making me his *pet*, just like he said.

His tail slides between my legs, taking my underwear down my thighs. I shiver, utterly captivated by his touch, his words, his *commanding presence*.

He stares down at me, his black irises swirling with crimson flares. "Am I going to have to compel you to behave, Viviana?"

I swallow, somewhat distracted by his question. "Strigoi can compel? Like vampires?"

His eyebrow arches, his fingers seeming to flex in my hair as his opposite hand reaches my panties, which are being held up by that sharp triangle tip. He grabs the fabric and brings it to his nose, his gaze temporarily shadowing as he closes his eyes.

Oh God. My thighs clench.

This isn't… this isn't…

I don't…

I expected a powerful vampire. An alluring one. A reclusive creature I would only see from afar, snap a few photos of, and… and *document* in my thesis.

Not *this*.

Not some fantasy out of one of Gaby's books.

Maybe I'm dreaming, I think, bewildered.

But, God, I hope not.

I want this to be real.

To be here. *With him.*

Even if I am on my knees and peering up into a pair of narrowed eyes.

He tucks my underwear into his pocket, then strokes my chin with his thumb.

"There will be no asinine questions, pet," he murmurs. "In fact, I think it best if you only part those pretty lips when I request use of your mouth."

Any other man saying that to me would have me wanting to punch him in the groin.

But this isn't a man.

He's a monster.

One I happen to have a lot of questions for, so I arch a brow. "That rule isn't going to work for me."

His long lashes flutter, a flash of surprise crossing his features. "You speak as though the rules are negotiable."

"All rules are negotiable."

"Not between us." The light touch on my face turns harsh as he pinches my chin. "I'm your king now, Viviana. The one you worship on your knees. The one you *serve*. Now tell me you understand."

My jaw clenches beneath his touch, my own gaze narrowing. The physical response is intrinsic. Asinine. And completely at odds with the tingling sensation warming my insides.

However, my mind has finally woken up, the thrall of meeting this creature slowly disintegrating behind a fresh, cool wave of reality.

As I told Marius earlier, I understood the potential consequences of meeting a monster. But I never actually cared.

Because the reward has always been worth the risk.

That hasn't changed.

Which is why I grab his wrist now—the one connected to the hand holding my jaw—and very clearly say, "*No*."

I won't *tell him I understand*.

I won't *obey*.

And I will not *serve* him.

"You might be a Strigoi King, but I haven't agreed to be your anything," I go on. "So if you expect me to *behave*, then I need to have a say in the rules. Otherwise, I'll simply refuse to cooperate. And then you'll have to compel me, which would be so incredibly depressing."

His brow furrowed while I spoke, his eyes seeming to search mine.

So I decide to add one more statement before he delivers whatever verdict is brewing inside that ancient head of his.

"Please don't disappoint me by taking the easy route, King Negru. It'll degrade everything I've learned about you over the years, and I really don't want that vision destroyed by something as boring as *compulsion*."

CHAPTER SIX
CIPRIAN

THIS FEMALE HAS RENDERED me speechless.

I expected acquiescence.

Fear.

A need to please.

Yet she's defying me from her knees, telling me not to compel her… because it will *disappoint* her.

Not because she's terrified. Not because she realizes I can merely take what I want. But because she doesn't want me choosing the path of least resistance.

Or, as she put it, *taking the easy route*.

I'm torn between ripping her pretty head off… and kissing the fuck out of her.

Confusion is not an emotion I'm well accustomed to experiencing. Witnessing, yes. Often, in fact. Especially when a human sees my wings. But feeling it myself? No.

However, this woman has me utterly flummoxed as to how to proceed.

Where most mortals bore me in a matter of seconds, this one has managed to ensnare my attention for several very long minutes. Years, honestly, if I include the time I've spent studying her research patterns.

My heart actually beats in my chest, my insides warm with the realization that this female has more than lived up to my expectations and desires. And I've barely even touched her.

Using my grip in her hair and on her chin, I pull her upward, my tail wrapping around her lower back to provide support as she stands. "I shall feed you now," I tell her, pleased with our progress.

Pleased… and frustrated.

But not dissatisfied. If anything, I'm quite the opposite. She's intriguing. I'm not sure that's an adjective I've ever associated with a human.

I've always compelled my meals to merely accept their fates, as it allowed for a faster embrace whereby I fed until full, wiped their memories, and then released them back into the wild.

Simple.

Easy, I realize, my gaze narrowing a bit. *Fucking easy*.

How have I never considered that before?

Why did it take meeting this little researcher to make me see that?

Is that why I've never been enthralled by my meals before? Why I never possessed a desire to fuck one of them?

I glance over my new pet, the way her dress clings to her curves—curves I now know are naked beneath the fabric—and decide that I'm nowhere near at risk of losing my desire in this situation.

Because I'm hard.

And I've been hard since the moment she entered my nest.

It's painful. But I embrace that pain because it means I'm feeling something. It means I *want* something—*someone*.

Which makes all of this worth it.

If she wants me to do this the hard way, I'll oblige.

However, it's going to end with her on her knees again by the end of the night.

With my cock in her mouth. In her cunt. In her ass. Wherever the fuck I want to take her, she'll accept it. Because that's why she's here. She's *mine*. My pet. My toy. My *female*.

Maybe I'll even breed her.

That notion means food is even more important, thus reminding me that I just told her about my intention to provide her with sustenance. Yet I'm still holding her to me like it's her I intend to devour first.

Hmm.

I lean down to run my nose against hers, loving the way she smells. The scent of her pussy still clings to my senses, that citrusy delight making my mouth water. I originally intended to throw her cotton undergarment into a nearby flame. But the aroma coming from the fabric caused me to smell it instead.

And now I'm keeping the item as a token.

A token of what, I'm not sure.

I just knew I couldn't discard it as I originally intended.

The tip of my tail runs around her side as I continue to hold her against me with my appendage wrapped around her lower back. She fits nicely here.

Perhaps I'll hold her while she eats.

The concept of releasing her doesn't quite suit.

So yes, that's how we'll proceed.

"You will sit in my lap." It's not a request but a demand. And if she chooses to question me, I'll force her to comply with my tail between her legs.

Is that a more interesting route *for you, darling pet?* I nearly ask aloud. *No compulsion. Just my tail forcing you to obey.*

"Okay," she breathes, her acquiescence almost displeasing me.

Because I rather liked the image of making her sit with me with my tail inside her.

Maybe I'll do it anyway.

It would be easy, I think, the triangle tip gliding down to her hip toward the high slit in her gown. It slides inside without hesitation, heading toward the treasure between her thighs.

"I think I will stroke you while you eat," I tell her, my voice lowering to a deep growl as a wave of feminine warmth travels up my appendage. It's unlike anything I've ever felt. It's a hot welcome. An invitation. A sweet kiss of perfection.

Her legs clench, trapping my tail before I can venture higher, her hands suddenly on my shoulders. But she doesn't deny me, just digs her nails into my jacket and holds on.

"Yes, this is how you will eat," I decide aloud. "And I will feed myself your pleasure."

My nose is still near hers, placing our mouths so close that I can almost taste her. She releases an unsteady exhale, her body seeming to roll even more into mine. Or maybe I pulled her closer. I'm not sure, but I suddenly need to see what her lips feel like beneath my own.

There's no reason for me not to find out.

She's mine. I've established that. And while she may want to discuss the rules, there will be no negotiation.

I will have her however I want. Wherever I want. *Whenever* I want.

Closing the small gap between us, I press my mouth to hers and wait. I'm not unfamiliar with the concept of a kiss. I've witnessed thousands, never quite understanding the point. There are so many better uses for feminine lips.

Though, as I hover against hers now, I begin to comprehend the allure of such a soft embrace.

It's a precursor to more.

A temptation.

An appetizer.

My tongue slips inside, curious to experience her unique flavor, and all I taste is mint.

"Hmm," I hum, not sure if I like that or not. I want to experience *her*, not the toothpaste in her room.

Perhaps it will be better to kiss her while fucking her, turn my little human into an animal of need and then devour her with my tongue.

Or maybe all I really want is to feast on her cunt.

She jumps as I push my tail upward, easily escaping her clenched thighs, and reach her weeping heat.

Gods, she's so fucking wet…

My tip easily glides through her slick pussy, right to the heart of her as I push inside her tight little hole.

She squirms and releases a protest, but I hold her with ease.

"Shh, pet," I hush. "I've never done this before, and I don't want to accidentally hurt you."

Pain is meant to be purposeful. It's the only way to derive true pleasure.

Which means she needs to let me play. Explore. *Learn.*

"*Negru.*" Her grasp on my shoulders tightens, her body seeming to freeze in shock. But then I find something inside her that has her melting into me as an adorable moan escapes her mouth. It's a beautiful hum against my lips, one that has me wanting to kiss her again.

So I do.

Because I can.

She jolts as I play with that spot I found inside her, her body seeming to shake against mine as I part her lips with my tongue once more.

The mint seems less powerful now, just refreshing, as I better acquaint myself with her mouth, all while exploring the tightness of her inner channel.

It's good that I used my tail first—my cock would not fit like this. She'll need to be stretched to accommodate me.

That's fine.

I'll enjoy the process.

In fact, we'll start now, I decide as I twirl my tip inside her and flare the triangle out just a little bit.

She startles and tries to pull away from me, so I band her lower back with my arm while my opposite hand slides down from her hair to her nape. Then I lift her off the ground and carry her to the chair.

Her mouth leaves mine on a yelp as I sit with her astride me, my tail still lodged between her legs. Originally, I intended for her to face the table while I fed her, but this works better for us both, as I'll be able to feed myself more easily as she comes.

"You will eat," I tell her, my lips close enough to hers to feel her resulting gasp. "And you will learn how to take me." I don't elaborate on what that means, just flare my tail again, which has her arching backward toward the table. "I don't want to injure you, pet. Not permanently, anyway."

"What about rules?" she manages to ask, her tone breathless. "We haven't—"

"I'll tell you the rules while you eat."

"That's not—"

"It's not a negotiation, Viviana." I stroke that place she clearly likes and almost smile when her eyes roll into the back of her head. That *is* an amusing little spot. Helpful, too. "You've been stalking me for years. Yet you still chose to come here. That's basically consent."

Her eyes widen. "You knew?"

"Of course I knew," I say, releasing her so I can reach around her to the table. "Why do you think I let you visit?" I pause then, my gaze leaving her mouth to focus on her eyes. "Or did you think you were clever enough to sneak up on me?"

Her brow puckers, the expression one I'm not sure I care for. But before I can comment on it, she says, "It's not about being clever. I just didn't expect someone in your standing to notice."

I stare at her. "Protecting my existence is how I survive, pet. Of course I *noticed*."

"So you wanted me here?"

"Obviously," I mutter, instantly bored by the trajectory of this conversation.

I renew my efforts to remove the lids from the food items on the table behind her, needing her to eat. Sustenance creates energy, and she's going to need her strength if she's going to survive me tonight.

"No, I mean, you plan—"

I swirl my tail inside her, done with the inane babbling. "The only sounds I want to hear from you are moans," I tell her, cutting off whatever she intended to say. Because I just don't care.

She obliges me with a throaty growl instead, one that has my cock throbbing in response.

"That is also acceptable," I inform her, my voice lower than before. "Now open your mouth so I can feed you."

Her eyes widen in response, yet her lips remain closed.

"Hmm, such a disobedient pet." It should irritate me.

But instead, I'm enthralled. Because she's making this interesting.

No, she's making it… *difficult.*

Not easy.

Not straightforward.

But *fun*.

I bring a fork up to her lips, the item on the end some sort of vegetable. She glances at it and jolts as I continue playing between her legs.

"Eat, Viviana," I demand.

She clenches her jaw, her gaze narrowing.

My eyebrow lifts. "Defying me, pet?"

Her hands are still on my shoulders, her nails seeming to dig even more into the fabric of my coat. "I can't eat like this."

I very nearly shoved the food into her mouth while she spoke. Hearing her words makes me wish that I had.

Alas, I was too busy watching her lips move to consider it fully.

"I will be most displeased if you break before I'm done using you, Ms. Dalca. Therefore, you're going to need to learn how to properly multitask." I remove my arm from her back so I can grab her chin again. "Now stop testing my patience and let me feed you."

CHAPTER SEVEN
VIVI

The tip of his tail is inside me.

It's thick. Softer than I expected. And it keeps *twirling*.

When he shushed me and told me that he's never done this before, I… I didn't know how to respond.

What does that even mean? I wonder, not for the first time.

He's never put his tail inside another woman?

I find that hard to believe, given how amazing it feels between my legs. He keeps stroking my G-spot, making my body burn for more. All while I'm shivering because *holy fuck, there's a tail inside me*.

This… this isn't natural.

Which is obvious. He's not human. He's a Strigoi.

And he has me in his lap… with a fork poised at my mouth.

The way his irises are flickering between obsidian and crimson tells me he's losing his patience—something he just warned me to *stop testing*.

God, this is insane. I'm not even hungry. But I open my mouth anyway because what the fuck else am I supposed to do?

He knew I was coming.

He knows about my research.

He wanted *me here*.

Those realizations all hit me within the last few minutes, my reality spinning wildly out of control.

I should be screaming. Demanding that he let me go. But instead, I'm chewing on… *broccoli*.

Ugh. I loathe broccoli. It's, like, the worst vegetable in existence, and I'm pretty sure my expression shows my feelings on the topic because he frowns.

"Have I harmed you?" he asks, his tail ceasing all movement inside me.

The unexpected question almost makes me choke on the food.

This monster is confusing. He demands that I obey him, basically forces himself inside me without requesting consent, yet pauses to express concern about my well-being. How am I supposed to react to that?

"I don't like broccoli," I admit after forcing myself to swallow. "Actually, I *despise* it."

Frown lines mar his brow. "I see." He releases my chin and wraps his arm around me again to pull me more firmly against him.

Which causes his tail to go deeper.

And makes me shudder in response.

Because oh. My. God.

I'm pretty sure eight inches of him are inside me now, which is a lot longer and thicker than anything else I've ever experienced.

I feel so full I could explode.

I should hate him. Hate *this*. But I haven't even tried to make him stop.

My obsession with this creature has clearly rendered me insane.

Can I truly be upset, though?

Especially when he can move like that…?

My eyes roll back in my head as that triangle tip flares again, stretching me inside in a way I've never experienced before. Definitely not a common sensation. At least, not for me.

But wow. I… I don't think I mind this. Even though I should. And I—

"What about pasta?" he asks, his voice low and near my ear.

At some point in the last minute, I curled myself into his chest and pressed my face against his neck. I didn't even realize it, too lost to the pleasure ripping through my insides.

Or maybe he compelled me.

I can be upset about that potential reason later.

Because right now, all I care about is the warmth pooling in my belly. *He's going to make me come.*

"I…" I swallow, unable to focus on what he's asked or anything other than the heat growing inside me. It's being stoked by the pressure against my G-spot. And the… the *thickness* of his appendage… it's… *Oh God…*

Everything goes dark, then bright, and my world detonates in a cloud of euphoria that threatens to annihilate me.

It's intense.

It's unworldly.

It's *insanity*.

The Strigoi King releases a low rumbling growl that has me shuddering against him as his tail continues to move inside me. My grasp on reality shifts, my mind seeming to blank entirely. I have no idea where I am. Who I am. What I'm doing.

Just feeling.

Hearing.

Breathing.

The growing pressure inside me that makes me see stars, his tail doing something I can't define. I know it's swirling. But it's getting impossibly bigger. *That triangle tip…* He's still stretching me. And I'm pretty sure I'm going to be bruised later as a result.

But then the sensation lessens, and his presence disappears from between my legs.

A whimper escapes me, the needy sound one I don't think I've ever made before. Given that I've never done anything like this before either, I shouldn't be surprised or embarrassed, yet warmth crawls up my neck regardless.

I'm a mess, I think, bewildered by the last… *God, has it even been thirty minutes?*

None of this is what I anticipated from this meeting. Though, I'm not sure what I truly expected. All my plans ended with finding the vampire and confirming he exists.

A myriad of consequences rolled through my mind, but none of them could thwart my desire to locate this male.

Including the potential consequence of death.

Which I guess makes me suicidal.

But I had to know the truth. It was like a compulsion that dictated the meaning of life.

"Mmm, you taste even better than you smell, pet," King Negru says, his low, heated words drawing me back just enough to look up at him.

The tip of his tail is against his lips.

The tip that was just inside me.

My thighs clench in response, the very real visual nearly sending me spiraling again.

"I can't believe this is happening," I whisper, more to myself than to him.

His eyes meet mine, and I swear I see a ghost of a

smile cross his features, but then his stoic mask returns. "If you don't eat, I will hurt you. And that's unacceptable to me."

I blink, his tone harsh and utterly unexpected. "Are you threatening me?"

He stares at me, his brow furrowing a bit. "Yes, I'm a threat to you. That's why I need you energized. So stop disobeying me and *eat*."

"I'm not *disobeying*," I tell him. "I'm *overwhelmed*."

"Hmm," he hums. "How very human of you."

"Because I'm a human," I snap back, starting to feel more like myself again. Whatever *that* even means.

I'm bewildered. I'm excited. I'm *thoroughly* pleased. And… *Ugh!* I cannot believe I just let him do that to me.

Using my hands on his shoulders, I push myself upright. It does little to restore my dignity since I'm straddling his lap with my dress bunched around my hips—thanks to his tail—and completely exposed.

However, I ignore that and force myself to meet his burning gaze. "You know about my research." It's not a question but a statement. "You know who I am."

His jaw ticks. "This is a boring conversation. Either eat or I'll move on to fucking you."

I narrow my gaze. "I haven't consented to that."

Or to you putting your tail between my legs, I think.

Though, I don't add that part out loud since the evidence of my enjoyment is still glistening near his mouth.

"Kings don't require consent."

"Of course they don't," I mutter. "So you're going to compel me?"

He cants his head as his tail trails up my leg again. "I think I just proved that compulsion isn't required to ensure your compliance, pet."

I try to move, to close my thighs, to do *something* to stop him, but his arm is steel against my back again as his triangle tip finds my entrance and pushes inside.

A startled gasp escapes me at the intrusion, because he's instantly stretching me again, and I swear he's forcing me to take even more than before. "*That burns*," I hiss at him, trying futilely to escape his hold.

But he drags me closer until his mouth is hovering against mine. "Stop squirming," he demands. "I already warned you once that I'm new to this, and I will be most displeased if you make me hurt you."

"I'm not *making* you do anything," I grind out, my eyes threatening to close at the sensations ripping through my body.

God, I hate how good that feels.

It's hot. It's rhythmic. *It's so fulfilling.*

"You're… you're *making* me…" I can't finish the statement, my heart pounding too loud for me to hear. "*Please…*" I'm not sure if I want him to stop or keep going.

It's too much.

He's putting too much inside me.

Expanding me too severely.

His lips brush mine as he whispers something I can't hear over the thudding in my ears. Then I feel air in my mouth, like he's forcing me to inhale every part of him.

Instinctually, I do exactly that, his calming lavender scent filling my senses and lulling me into a state of utter confusion.

I'm in pain. Yet I'm… I'm elated.

I'm soothed.

I'm writhing with *heat.*

I don't know what he's doing to me, but it's shattering my hold on reality.

And, abruptly, I'm flying.

Except his wings are still tucked at his back and we're

seated in the chair. It's just the perception of being in flight that I'm experiencing.

Because I'm climaxing again.

It shouldn't be possible.

I've *never* been able to come like this.

Holy wow…

I black out. Or I think I do. I'm… I'm not really sure.

But suddenly my back is against something hard, and I'm staring up at the ceiling.

And King Negru… he's… he's… I squint, my head barely lifting off of whatever I'm lying on—the table, maybe?—to see his dark head disappearing between my thighs.

There are dishes everywhere. Food. Shattered glass.

Definitely still in the dining room.

What is he…?

My lips part as something velvety strokes between my folds. Something wet. Something distinctly like… *a tongue.*

When his mouth seals around my clit and sucks, I buck upward, the wooden surface beneath me allowing me to glide with ease.

Until his palm pushes me back down.

"No moving," he growls, the vibration of those words traveling through my nerve endings and setting me on fire. "I want to do this properly, pet."

Everything he's saying, everything he's doing… it's…

Oh, hell.

I'm done thinking.

I'm done trying to process what's happening to me.

I walked into a monster's home to find out if he existed. Now I know the truth. And it's time to face the consequences of my choices.

If he wants to *devour* me like he claimed, then I'm helpless to stop him. I may as well—

A scream leaves my mouth as something sharp pierces my intimate flesh.

His fangs, I realize, suddenly on fire inside and out.

His hand holds me down as he… as he *swallows*.

Garbled sounds escape me as the world shifts in and out of focus.

It *burns*.

But a strange sort of euphoria chases the scorching flames, a rapture that has me gasping for air as I claw through a sea of intense oblivion.

It's like an orgasm, only harsher and all-consuming.

Now I'm not just flying—I'm *soaring*. Into space. Into another orbit of existence.

I think I say his name. I may even cry for him to stop. I… I don't know. I can't…

Darkness pulls at me, my limbs going cold.

He's killing me, I realize. *Drinking from between my thighs… driving me into a rapturous universe… only to drown me in death.*

Tears track down my cheeks, the sensation resembling ice.

I'm not sad. I'm… I'm something else entirely. Accepting? Disappointed? Longing for more? It's impossible to decide.

Nothing makes sense here.

Yet everything feels strangely right.

His growls are all I hear now.

The exquisite agony of his bite is all I feel.

And a starless sky… is all… I see.

CHAPTER EIGHT
CIPRIAN

Fuck, she tastes amazing.

Her blood. Her pussy. Her *ecstasy*.

I've seen females come before. But this is my first time being the cause of a woman's pleasure. The first time I've actually understood the allure of watching a partner fall apart. The first time I've ever desired to indulge in the experience and feel the orgasm for myself.

Only it's my fingers in her cunt now as she climaxes for me.

She's no longer awake, just living in a dream of ecstasy.

It's dangerous. Her heartbeat is less steady. Her breaths are shallow.

I need to stop feasting.

To stop drinking.

To stop forcing pleasure from her exquisite form.

But I want more. I'm not ready to give her a break. I need her to keep up. To *live*. To do this for hours, days, weeks, maybe even months.

And I want it to happen while my cock is in her slick warmth. Deep inside her. *Where I belong…*

My shaft throbs, my balls demanding that I take action. Strip myself. Shove myself into her wet pussy. *And fuck.*

Except I need her to be awake for the experience. Watch her eyes as I make her fall apart over and over. Hear her delicious screams. Her cute little whimpers.

Gods, I'm obsessed.

I lick her again, loving her citrusy flavor. It's tainted with her blood. That decadent mixture is my new favorite drink. A blossoming addiction.

Only, it's not as lively as it was before.

Because my pet is dying.

I growl. "*This* is why I needed you to eat," I tell her, irritated that she didn't obey.

But I'm even more annoyed with myself because I lost control and rushed the experience.

Feeling her clench around my tail for a second time proved to be too much for my patience.

I stood with her in my arms, then spread her out on the table.

Food and drinks were lost.

All I wanted was her.

So I ripped up her dress and pressed my mouth to her cunt… and sank my fangs into her clit.

I told myself I would be satisfied with a few swallows.

It was a lie.

Looking at her now, I realize I've taken far too much. More than I've ever demanded of my prey.

She's going to die.

I stand between her lifeless legs, studying her trimmed mound and the mingling essence painting her pretty pussy lips.

My tail caresses her calf before traveling higher, my heart seeming to hammer in my rib cage.

This sight captivated me before, made my inner beast

roar with triumph and need. So I fed. I indulged. But now…

I swallow.

I'm no longer captivated. I'm devastated.

We've only just begun.

She can't fucking die yet.

This female is the first one I've ever desired to do more to than bite. The first female I've ever licked or pleasured or *experienced* in any other way than a quick strike to the neck.

She tastes divine. Like a bright, beautiful day. A renewed existence. *Citrus trees bathing in the afternoon sun.*

"No." It comes out on a snarl of sound. "*No.* I do not accept this, pet."

She will live.

She will eat.

She will prepare herself for me.

And she will fucking survive everything I want to do to her.

Lifting my wrist to my mouth, I sink my fangs into the skin and *rip*.

Then I push the gushing wound to her mouth. "Fucking drink," I demand. "Then you're going to sleep this off, and we'll try again in the morning."

Because I will be enjoying her for breakfast, lunch, and dinner. And anything else I desire in between.

When her throat doesn't move like it should, I wrap my palm around her nape and drag her lifeless body up off the table. She feels fragile in my arms, the sensation at odds with the feisty temperament she exuded earlier.

My lips flatten. "I'm displeased, pet." I hold her against me, bite my wrist again just to ensure it doesn't heal, and press it to her mouth once more. "*Drink.*"

This time, I lace compulsion through the word. It's

intrinsic. Natural. Yet makes me wince inside because I can hear her expressing disappointment at me choosing an "easy" method for forcing her compliance.

Well, I prefer that over her dying.

So if she wants to chastise me once she wakes, I'll allow it.

Then I'll kiss her and fuck her against the wall.

Hmm, no, I think. *No, I'll make her eat first.*

Or perhaps I'll feed her my cock and give her my cum as an appetizer.

I consider that option as I watch her slender throat move. Instead of blood, I imagine it's my masculine essence. Coating her insides. Bathing her in my presence. My *claim*.

I've never desired such an experience.

But with her, I would easily enjoy marking her in that way.

I shift my palm from her nape to the back of her head, loving the way her silky strands feel against my skin.

She truly is beautiful. Petite, too. Intelligent. *Unique*.

"You're an ideal pet," I inform her softly. "I like that you don't fear me." Of course, that may change now that I nearly killed her. But I hope not. "I didn't intend to hurt you." I mean it. "I got carried away."

She can't hear me.

However, my words are not really for her. I just feel like I need to voice them, to make everything clear. Perhaps more to myself than to Viviana. I'm… I'm not quite sure.

This is unprecedented.

I knew she was different the moment I learned of her existence. But I never dreamed she would live up to my expectations for her.

Fuck, I'm rather certain she *surpassed* them.

Which is asinine, as I've barely had my fill of her.

She passed out too quickly.

"Next time I tell you to eat, you will listen," I inform her flatly. "That may not have saved you tonight, but it would have helped you last a little longer."

In theory, anyway.

Although, I did drink a lot. More than I ever have before. Yet I still feel parched. Specifically, for *her*.

"We will work up to this together," I decide out loud. "You will learn how to take me, and I will learn how to… pace myself."

That feels like a reasonable compromise.

I study her face, noting the way the color has returned to her cheeks.

She's still drinking, which isn't truly necessary, but I rather like the way her mouth feels against my wrist.

My immortality will renew her strength, make her less breakable, and perhaps even create other, interesting effects.

This won't *turn* her. That's a lore that exists for vampire kind. Strigoi must be born. But blood exchange like this is a mating practice.

If I feed her two more times, she will become mine.

My gaze roams over her, my mind forming a picture of our potential future.

As my mate, she would bear my heirs.

"Mmm," I hum, tracking my gaze down over her breasts, which are shapely and plump beneath the dress, to her flat abdomen. "I think I rather like the idea of you growing with my seed inside you." It would claim her as mine in a whole new way. Plus, the breeding part would be most enjoyable.

With her, I think, my cock hardening again.

My erection finally waned after seeing her almost dead on the table. But now my need returns with renewed vigor, the idea of forcing my seed to take root inside her making me want to rouse her and tell her to run, just so I can hunt her like prey.

"Fuck, pet," I whisper, still staring at her torso and imagining her carrying our child. "You're bewitching."

I finally remove my wrist from her mouth, then lean down to lick her lips clean. She responds by kissing me, her body automatically answering my call, just as it should.

Though, she's still very much asleep.

"If you didn't need rest, I would start breeding you right now," I say against her mouth. "But you definitely require energy if I'm going to impregnate you."

Saying it aloud makes my stomach clench with desire.

"We'll see how much you can take tomorrow, Ms. Dalca. Test your limits. Determine if you're worthy of a hunt." I kiss her once more, dip my tongue into her mouth just to renew my claim there, then rearrange her in my arms so I can easily stand.

She curls into me, like she's seeking my warmth and comfort.

It's a movement that would normally have me dropping a mortal to the floor. But with her, I rather like it, so I purr for her in response.

It's another instinctual reaction on my part, one reserved for a mate.

If Marius heard it, he would be duly startled—perhaps even more so than if I were to smile in his presence.

Well, it shocks me, too. Though, it shouldn't. This female has intrigued me for years. Of course, I'm even more obsessed with her now that I finally have her in my arms.

"I cannot tell you how pleased I am that you're continuing to fascinate me," I tell her. "I was worried my infatuation might come to an abrupt end. However, you've proven to be… delectable."

There are more words I would give her as praise, but I'm momentarily distracted in the kitchen as we pass through.

"Radu?" I say quietly, causing the intercom system to activate with an alert.

I wait.

"Yes, my lord?" a deep voice responds less than a minute later, the source of it coming from a speaker embedded in the ceiling.

"Can you please arrange an array of shelf-stable snacks and take them up to our guest's quarters?" I ask my manor manager. "I assume Ms. Dalca will wake up hungry, and I would prefer her to have easy access to some sustenance."

"I'll prepare a tray for her, my lord."

"Thank you, Radu," I say. "And please provide her with water as well."

"Of course, my lord."

I nod, satisfied that he will get the job done, and continue onward through the main level toward the grand staircase in the front foyer. Flaring my wings, I fly us up to the second-floor landing, then walk the rest of the way to my pet's quarters.

Her room already smells like her, all citrus with a subtle hint of spice—something I've only just begun to notice. *Arousal,* I recognize, more than familiar with that glorious fragrance now.

"You may not have realized your purpose in coming here, but your body more than accepted your fate, Ms. Dalca," I murmur as I lay her on the bed.

Her fragility has lessened, leaving behind a strong female.

"My immortality looks good on you," I inform her

softly. "As does this gown. Alas, you'll sleep more soundly in the nude." I lean down to rip the fabric off of her, then pause to admire her gorgeous form.

Her nipples are a luscious pink, the tips beading as though begging for my mouth.

Or perhaps she's already preparing for her purpose—*to be bred.*

An appreciative hum escapes me as I pull the remnants of the dress away from her, tossing all of the pieces to the floor. Then I bend over to kiss each breast.

"I think I'll bite you here next, pet." I drag my fangs across her peak, then lick the rosy tip. "Gods, you taste amazing."

For a moment, I imagine how heavy her tits will become when producing milk for our child.

It's a foreign fantasy, one I've never allowed myself to consider. Because I've never met someone I wanted to fuck, let alone impregnate.

But Viviana… she makes me want to dream.

I trace the underside of her breast with my finger, then test the weight of her plump flesh. It's already the perfect size. Though, pregnancy would change her.

"You'll just become even more stunning," I decide out loud. "We'll discuss it more in the morning, sweet intended." I close my mouth around her nipple, giving it a little suck, then kiss a path up to her throat to lave her steady pulse. "I can't wait to make your heart race again." The words are a whisper against her ear.

She shivers beneath my touch, so I shift her around on the bed and bundle her in the blankets.

"Rest, pet," I demand. "And wake up ready to obey. Or there will be consequences."

I brush my lips against her forehead, then leave her to dream of me.

Tomorrow, her training will begin.

It isn't easy being a Strigoi King's intended mate. There are expectations. Rules. Dutiful requirements.

And, most importantly, there are *trials*. Not organized by me, but by my constituents.

That's why I've been so selective about my companionship.

I need someone infallible. Someone unafraid of consequences. Someone willing to stand by my side.

Marius thought Viviana Dalca might be my "ticket home."

I scoffed at the concept earlier, claiming she wasn't a candidate.

But for the first time in centuries, I feel a glimmer of an emotion I thought long dead—*hope*.

Maybe Viviana is the one who will return me to my throne. Bear me an heir. Make me a true king.

Alas, the trials are not kind. They're deadly. A means of Strigoi entertainment. And they're not mine to manage.

If Viviana's marked as my intended, then she'll need to learn how to obey and assimilate. Or she'll never survive in my world.

She'll either become my mate and a Strigoi Queen.

Or she'll fail.

And die.

CHAPTER NINE
VIVI

Crunch. Crunch. Crunch.

The noise echoes through my head, making my brow furrow.

Crinkle.

Crunch. Crunch. Crunch.

My lips curl down. "Gaby?" I guess, barely awake. "Are you eating chips?" The question sounds groggy to my ears. I feel strange. Hungover, yet not.

And thirsty.

Very thirsty.

Peering toward my nightstand, I search for my usual bottle. Only… only my nightstand is not *my* nightstand. It's an ornate piece of furniture that I've never seen before.

Except, no. That's not true. It's…

My eyes fly open as a gasp leaves my mouth. *King Negru.* I'm in his castle.

In a guest suite.

And I'm alive.

I think, anyway.

My hands start roaming my body, searching for signs of death. But all I find is smooth skin.

Because I'm naked.

Very, *very* naked.

I'm also not alone in the room.

Because that crunching sound hasn't stopped, and neither has the crinkling.

Warily, I roll toward it, then gape at finding Marius lounging in a chair near the bed, his gaze on the windows. "Not Gaby," he murmurs, then glances at me. "You ready to head back to Brașov?"

I blink at him. "What?"

"Tour's over," he says. "Ciprian told me to take you back to your hotel. So once you're ready, we'll hit the road."

"Ciprian?" I echo, not sure who he's talking about. "Does King Negru know about this?"

"King Negru is Ciprian." Marius utters the words slowly, like he's explaining something to a child. "And he told me to escort you out first thing, but I'm a gentleman. Which is why I let you sleep." He checks his watch. "But we really should go before he realizes you're still here."

My brow furrows. "He wants me to leave?"

"That's what I said, isn't it?"

I sit up, then grasp for the sheets when I remember that I have nothing on, and glare at the male in my room. "Get out."

"Excuse me?"

"Get. Out." I enunciate the demand with acute precision, my tone flat. "And tell *Ciprian* that if he wants me to go, he can come say that to my face."

Because there is no way I am leaving this castle without having a stern word with him.

He can't just bite me and discard me. Not after… I don't…

Okay. He's a monster. A Strigoi King. I guess he can technically do whatever he wants. But that doesn't mean I'm going to merely accept this.

"Just to make sure we're clear—you're refusing to leave, right?" Marius asks, causing my gaze to narrow even more.

"I'm not going anywhere until I talk to Ciprian." It's probably not the wisest decision to demand an audience with the male who all but killed me last night.

But I'm not feeling all that intelligent this morning.

I'm feeling… elated. Furious. *Invincible.*

That final sensation isn't something I can describe. I simply feel alive in a way I never have before. And leaving is the absolute last thing I want to do.

"Excellent." Marius hops up to his feet, chip bag in hand. "I'll be sure to let His Majesty know." He starts toward the door, then pauses to say, "Thanks for making this easy, Ms. Dalca."

"Making what easy?" I ask as he heads through the threshold.

"Oh, and be ready in thirty minutes," he calls back to me. "Ciprian intends to have you for lunch."

The door slams before I can ask what he means by that.

Of course, after last night, I'm pretty sure *have you for lunch* is a direct description of future events.

Which leaves me frowning at the door.

He just told me Ciprian wants me to leave. And now he's saying the Strigoi King wants to eat me?

I shake my head, confused.

Then growl when I hear the snick of a lock, telling me I'm once again a prisoner in this room.

"That's not confusing at all," I say to no one in particular.

"You tell me to leave, then lock me inside. So which is it, *Strigoi King*? Do you want me gone? Or am I your captive?"

Okay, I guess I'm talking to *Ciprian*. But I doubt he can hear me.

Or maybe he's listening.

On the chance he is, I keep talking. "How about I tell you what I'm not going to be?" I pull the blankets off myself, determined to find something to wear. But I pause when I see the dried blood between my legs.

Memories of last night flash through my mind, how he held me down on the table and devoured my intimate flesh.

A wave of arousal warms my blood, the reaction one at odds with the skip in my pulse.

I thought I was dying.

Yet there's no evidence of my weakened state.

I simply feel rejuvenated, like I just experienced the best night of rest in my life.

That sensation of invincibility comes over me again as I move, my legs stronger than normal. Even my movements seem to be faster.

What did he do to me? I wonder, standing and spinning around in a quick circle. *Why do I feel like I could fly right now?*

It's strange. It's enlightening. It's otherworldly.

Despite the growing sense of insanity, I smile. "Not sure what's happening to me, but I like it."

Then I remember that I was talking to the Strigoi King.

Or pretending to, anyway.

And I was in the middle of saying what I'm not going to be. *Right.* "You want me for lunch? The answer is no, *my king*. We need to talk about the rules and the importance of consent first."

Bold words, I suppose. But they're important to say after last night.

I don't even know what happened.

His tail was there.

Followed by his mouth.

Did he fuck me? I look down, frowning. I'm not sore at all. Which is strange. After everything he did inside me with that triangle tip, I should feel something.

Well, regardless, I need to at least wash the blood off.

I start toward the bathroom, then pause at the tray on the table.

A tray full of snacks, including bags of chips.

Arching my brow, I thumb through it and grab a banana, as well as a water, and take them with me on my quest to the shower.

The rainfall pours over my head for a lot longer than thirty minutes, something I do on purpose because I want to defy Marius's statement, and also because it feels interesting.

It's like I can see the tiny droplets falling in slow motion. Such a bizarre realization, one that puts me under a strange sort of trance. The water gliding along my skin captivates me, too. The soothing sensation is hypnotic. Mesmerizing. *Wonderful.*

I trace a path down my arm, then giggle at the tingling feeling that follows.

Only for a growl to make all the hair dance against the back of my neck. "I do not like to be kept waiting, Ms. Dalca."

"Oh?" I draw out the word but don't look at him. "Well, I don't like waking up and being told to leave by a Strigoi's familiar."

I bend down and pick up a bottle, then read the French

label. Even without studying the language, I would still recognize the translation for *shampoo*.

Well, I haven't washed my hair yet, so I may as well do that now.

While the Strigoi King waits.

Opening the bottle, I lather the light pink liquid into my hair. It has a hint of strawberries to it that I find quite pleasant.

Of course, the scent of lavender and vanilla is stronger.

And it's coming from behind me.

"I also don't appreciate nearly bleeding out on a dining table," I go on as I move beneath the spray, my back still to the Strigoi King. "I'm not particularly fond of losing time or memories either." I utter the words while drawing my fingers through my hair. "And I strongly dislike being locked in a room when I've shown no desire to escape."

I finish rinsing the shampoo, then bend to pick up the conditioner.

A subtle growl echoes behind me, the owner of it obviously growing impatient.

Rather than acknowledge the sound, I say, "I'm not fond of rules without explanations, *Your Majesty*. So, if you want me to *behave*, you'll have to actually talk to me. Not fuck me with your tail. Not kiss me senseless or bite me. But *talk* to me."

I turn as I massage the conditioner into my scalp and finally meet the monster's obsidian gaze. It's practically burning with annoyance, little crimson flares flickering in the irises. "Are you done chastising me, *pet*?"

"Probably not," I sass back at him, feeling particularly confident.

Which makes no sense since Marius told me that *Ciprian* wants me to leave.

But maybe that just means I have nothing to lose.

If the Strigoi King has decided he's done with me, then I may as well give him a piece of my mind.

"There are much better uses for your mouth, Ms. Dalca," King Negru informs me. "Perhaps a lesson on your knees will remind you who and what I am."

"I'm staring at you right now, *Ciprian*," I say, using his first name mostly to piss him off, but also because I happen to like the way it sounds. "I know exactly who and what you are."

"Yet you speak to me as though we are equals," he returns.

"If we were equals, you would be as naked as I am right now. Not dressed in a freshly pressed suit while I shower in front of you," I point out, then step back to rinse the conditioner from my hair while he watches.

I can't see him since my eyes are closed, but I can feel his gaze on me like a burning caress against my skin. It's both a welcome sensation and a chilling one. Because I can't tell if he's thinking about devouring me again or outright killing me.

Perhaps a bit of both.

Turning, I go to find a shower gel or something to clean off my skin. I meant to focus on the area between my thighs, but I hesitate now.

Will that be too much? I wonder, frowning.

Then I give myself a mental shrug. *Nothing to lose, remember?*

King Negru growls again, the sound echoing through the oversized shower as I use a soap bar—I couldn't find any gel—to start cleaning myself.

"Are you trying to tempt me, pet?" he asks.

"I didn't invite you in to watch," I return. "So no. I'm merely trying to get rid of the aftermath from last night." I face him again. "Which is another thing I don't like—I don't like waking up with dried blood between my legs. It's uncomfortable."

He leans against the glass—there isn't a shower door, just an open space large enough for him to walk through with his wings. But he doesn't do that. He stays about five feet away from me, only further highlighting how large this shower is.

"Anything else you want to tell me?" he asks, and I can tell by his flat tone and his bored expression that he's not actually interested in what I have to say.

Which naturally only makes me want to talk more.

And more than that, I want to surprise him.

"I enjoyed your tail between my legs," I admit.

His nostrils flare in response, breaking his stoic countenance. It's a minute change, but enough to encourage me to continue speaking.

"I think asking for permission next time might be a good idea, though," I add.

"Permission?" he echoes.

"Yes." I trail the bar of soap along my lower stomach and downward to my shaved mound. "Acquiring my consent ensures my enthusiastic participation, Ciprian."

"You were more than *enthusiastic* last night, Viviana."

I shiver, the way my name rolls off his tongue resembling a seductive purr. "Was I enthusiastic after nearly bleeding out on the table?"

His brow furrows a little. "You're healed."

"That's not the point." I set the soap bar aside and rinse myself off, then saunter toward him, uncaring that I'm completely naked. "Wouldn't you rather I be a willing participant while you fuck me?"

"I didn't fuck you last night." He straightens to tower over me as we square off in the shower threshold. "I want to hear you scream while I use you, pet."

"Then ask me for consent so I can give you what you want."

He arches a brow. "You've already given me consent, Viviana. You're in my castle. My world. *My nest.* Marius offered you a chance to leave, and you refused. Therefore, you have chosen to remain here as my toy, thus making your intentions clear."

My lips part, a correction lining my tongue, but suddenly I'm on my knees in the shower and staring straight up at him like last night.

I'm so stunned I can barely feel the pain echoing up my limbs from the abrupt movement.

Or maybe it's because I'm distracted by his tail—which I belatedly realize is how I ended up in this position.

The appendage slips free from my back, the triangle tip brushing my side before gliding up my torso toward my throat.

"There will be no more talking," he tells me, his tail wrapping around my neck like a collar as he begins to unzip his pants. "The only sounds I want to hear are the ones of you choking on my cock."

CHAPTER TEN
CIPRIAN

She stayed.

And not just that, but she refused to even consider leaving.

Watching her talk to Marius both irked me and pleased me. Irked me because she was naked beneath the sheets. Pleased me because she didn't even hesitate in issuing her response.

She sounded like a queen. *My* queen.

Which means she passed her first test—one born of courage. Had Viviana opted to leave, I may have allowed it. But deep down, I knew she wouldn't be able to accept my best friend's offer.

Because she's different.

She doesn't fear me.

She *challenges* me.

This mortal—this petite female who is a foot shorter than my six-foot-four frame—glares up at me with fierceness that has my cock throbbing with need.

This is what I've been missing for centuries. This sense of equality. Which is ironic, given that I just criticized her for speaking to me as though I were her equal, then threatened to put her on her knees like this to teach her a lesson on the topic.

But what I don't admit aloud is that she's already acting like a Strigoi Queen.

She *criticized* me. Told me everything that displeased her. Then dared to demand that I request consent.

I could.

I might.

However, not now. Not in this moment. Because I need her to learn when to bow.

And most importantly, I need her to understand where the power exists in this relationship.

Because while I might be the one towering over her right now, I'm the one in a vulnerable position. I want to feel her mouth around me. I want to experience bliss… *with her*.

A first.

A dream I've never allowed myself to indulge in.

But I'm trusting her to share this with me. To be my *partner* in this sensual journey.

She has no idea how important this is or that she's actually the one with the control here. I could truly force her, coerce her with my mind, make her swallow me whole.

Yet I'm not doing that at all.

I've said the words, threatened her by putting her on her knees, and told her what I desire.

Now it's up to her to follow through.

I reach through my zipper and pull my cock out, then watch as she takes in my size.

Her eyes widen. Her mouth parts. And I hear a little hitch of surprise.

When her gaze darts back up to mine, I merely arch a brow, daring her to speak again.

But all she does is dampen her lips with her tongue.

"Open your mouth, Viviana."

She surprises me by obeying, the simple motion making my dick throb with need.

"Wider," I tell her, needing to be sure I can enter her properly.

Again she does as I demand, her eyes holding mine the whole time.

"This is why words of consent are unnecessary," I inform her as I press the head of my cock to her full lips. "Actions are what matter, and right now, you're practically begging me to fuck that pretty mouth of yours."

Her gaze narrows a little, and I suspect she's about to try to speak.

So I push inside of her instead, silencing whatever she might say.

Her nostrils flare, her pupils dilating with a mixture of arousal and a hint of fear. Or maybe it's pain. I'm stretching her mouth with my girth. "Breathe, pet. I need to see how much of me you can take, and I don't want to accidentally suffocate you."

At least, not for too long.

I want my pet to survive, not die.

But I meant what I said about hearing her choke on my cock. Just the notion of it has my balls tightening as I slide deeper into her wet heat.

Her palms fist against her thighs, her shoulders seeming to tighten.

"Relax," I command. "I've never done this before, so I need to focus on not harming you. And I can't do that if you're tense."

Because panic is an aphrodisiac that risks my control.

My beast wants to rip her apart and bring her back with my blood. Use her for pleasure, then force her to come even while she's begging to breathe.

It's a violent craving, one I intend to work up to.

However, I need to learn how to do this first.

And that requires intense concentration, which is hard for me to maintain when I'm worried about her hurting herself in the process.

Questions seem to radiate from her eyes as she stares up at me, but her shoulders visibly relax for me. "Good girl," I murmur, pleased with both her acquiescence and the way she's taking my cock. "Gods, this feels incredible." Unlike anything I've ever experienced. She's so hot and wet. "Flatten your tongue."

She does.

Because she's made for this. Made for *me.*

And fuck if I don't feel like I could already come.

I'm not even halfway inside her, my length far too long for her to take to the hilt like this. But I have to know how deep I can go.

Slowly, I feed her more, only pausing when I feel her tense again.

Pulling back just slightly, I say, "Inhale deeply for me, princess. I'm going to keep pushing, so you're going to need to hold your breath."

She swallows instead, the action sending a jolt down my spine.

Gods, I had no idea it could feel like *this*.

Now I want to shove myself down her throat and demand that she swallow again and again.

But I wait until she pulls enough air into her lungs before resuming my exploration.

I don't rush. I simply press, forcing her to embrace my thickness and stealing her ability to breathe.

A lush note of fear spices her citrusy scent, causing my beast to roar in approval. I want more of that. More of her. More of this feeling.

So. Fucking. Good.

My eyes nearly close, but I have to keep watching her. To protect her while I take my pleasure from her sweet little mouth.

Threading my fingers through her hair, I hold her in place, then take hold of her jaw to tug down on her chin. "Wider, pet."

Her gaze tells me that's impossible.

But I need her to try.

"I want to feel your throat, so you're going to have to take more, Viviana."

She tries to shake her head.

"Don't reject me," I murmur, holding myself steady in her mouth. "Your body can take this. Trust me."

She swallows again, and I nearly come in response.

Focus, I remind myself. She's been holding her breath for at least thirty seconds. If I came now, I would literally drown her.

Which sounds fun in theory.

But I need her alive to properly enjoy her. Besides, I rather like Ms. Dalca and her feistiness. She spoke to me earlier without any concept of reverence. It was refreshing. Interesting. *Different.*

I stroke my thumb along her jaw, feeling her muscles contract as she tries futilely to open wider for me.

"You're such an obedient pet like this," I muse, pleased. Then I draw myself out to where I know she can breathe and instruct her to inhale again.

She does, and sweet tears begin to glisten in her dark eyes.

"So pretty," I tell her, thrusting into her mouth to meet the back of her throat.

She makes a cute little noise, one that almost sounds like choking.

"Careful, pet. You need your air." I make her take more, my grip on her hair unyielding as she tries to pull back. "Shh, I already told you that I don't want to hurt you. So let me learn how to fuck your mouth, Viviana."

I move my hips, pulling out just a little, then go even deeper on my next stroke. "*Fuuuck.*" Her throat gets tighter the more I push, which feels fucking incredible. "Gods, this is amazing."

Why have I gone my whole existence without experiencing this?

Because I've been waiting for her. Waiting for this.

My thumb catches a tear as it falls from her eye, and I bring the drop to my mouth.

Her nostrils flare again, but she can't breathe. I'm choking her, and I have no desire to stop. The way she's contracting around me is rapturous. So much so that I try to shove more into her mouth.

She squirms in response, her eyes going wide when her movements drive me into her throat. True pain blossoms across her features, making me growl in annoyance.

I shift and let her breathe again, but just barely because I don't want to leave the sanctity of her mouth. "Stop panicking," I demand.

She grabs my thighs, her nails digging into my skin through the thin fabric of my pants.

"You will calm down," I tell her. "Or you will kneel like this for hours." Because I'm not letting her go. Not now. Not *ever*.

A fiery emotion takes over her gaze, one that has my stomach clenching with excitement.

I like that look on her face. It's beautiful and made all the more alluring with her lips wrapped around my cock.

"Inhale, princess," I say, the words more of a warning than a demand. "I want you to focus on breathing while I play."

I don't give her a moment to agree, just push forward and cut her off mid-breath. Her pupils dilate, that fierce expression of hers seeming to intensify.

I admire it while indulging in the urge to *move*. It's a natural inclination, one that drags her tongue along the bottom of my shaft as I establish a rhythm in her mouth.

"Mmm," I hum appreciatively. "You might not be able to take me to the hilt this way, but it still feels fucking good, pet." I start to move faster, only to freeze as she hollows her cheeks around me. "*Fuck.* Do that again."

She doesn't.

Instead, she swallows.

Then arches a brow at me.

I glare down at her. "Suck me again, Viviana."

For the longest moment, she ignores my demand, and I nearly shove my cock down her throat in reprimand. But then she gives the slightest suck and tries to pull backward.

I almost stop her. However, curiosity has me lessening my hold to see what she'll do.

Her suction grows more intense as she draws me out to the tip. I nearly curse, furious and elated, only to growl as she pushes herself back onto my cock and takes me willingly to the back of her throat.

My grasp almost drops entirely, my knuckles brushing her jaw now instead of trying to pry her mouth open more. And my fingers loosen in her hair.

But I don't release her. Primarily because I can't stop touching her.

She's driving me mad with her mouth, mastering me in a way I never knew I could be mastered.

My tail flicks, my need to find some semblance of control driving my instinct to touch her in return. So I do—by stroking the triangle tip up the inside of her thigh and going straight to her pussy.

Viviana jumps, my cock nearly falling out of her mouth. Though, my grip in her hair keeps her in place as I punch my hips forward at the same time my tail spears into her pussy.

A garbled scream vibrates my shaft, making me groan as I fill her mouth and her cunt at the same time. She tries to shove away from me, one hand on my thigh and the other suddenly gripping my tail.

I flare the triangle tip inside her and growl low in my chest. "Careful, Ms. Dalca. My restraint is already hanging on by a thread. If you make me hurt you, I will be most displeased."

Her dark eyes narrow.

And I glare right back at her.

"Stop testing the boundaries of my control and let me pleasure us both."

Her expression doesn't abate.

She just continues to glower at me.

"Be a good little pet and suck my cock again so I know that you understand me," I say, testing her obedience. Because right now, she looks more likely to bite me than to do what I ask.

Except her cheeks cave inward as she does exactly what I requested.

A curse leaves me, the sensation of her suction pairing nicely with the realization that my pet is obeying me. "So good," I whisper, my voice turning guttural from the influx of pleasure. "Now slide your touch toward the tip of my tail and start stroking me near your pussy."

I've never let anyone touch me like this. Not my cock *or* my tail. But this female isn't like the others. This female is *mine.*

And like the dutiful little pet she is, she adheres to my command.

"*Gods, Viviana.*" The tendons of my neck bulge as I try to swallow, my body pent up tighter than ever before. "Ride my tail. Pretend it's my cock. Make yourself come while I use your mouth."

I'm losing control. Losing sight of what I'm doing. Too caught up in the sensations to think. To process. To do anything other than feel.

Which isn't okay.

I have to protect my intended mate. Have to make sure I don't accidentally kill her. But *fuck*, this feels so good. So fucking right. *So perfect.*

She grips my tail tightly, stroking it in a way that goes straight to my groin. "Don't stop," I beg her, not ashamed at all to let her hear the need in my voice. The *plea* for more. "Suck, pet. Suck hard."

She does.

Gods, she's everything I've dreamed of and more.

A surge of arousal hits me as she swallows around the head of my cock. And that surge hits a crescendo when she presses her tongue to my shaft, somehow applying pressure and doing things I didn't even think to ask for.

She's done this before, I realize. *Fuck, she's been with other men...*

That notion—the very genuine reality of it—has me thrusting deep into her throat, my need to *mark* and *claim* overtaking everything else.

This female is *mine.* She will not remember anyone else.

Will not think of past lovers. Will never be with another male again.

Only me.

Always with me.

Her nails dig into my tail as she chokes around my girth, but I don't stop. I punish her with my movements, force her to take me, ensure my cock is the last one she ever fucking tastes, all while claiming her pussy with my tail.

I'm so deep inside both her holes that I'm all she can feel. All she can experience. All she can *take*.

She tries to pull back, her teeth touching my sensitive skin. But I refuse to release her. She's going to come for me. She's going to scream for me. And then she's going to swallow for me.

I tell her that out loud as I pump in and out of her mouth, my tail echoing the movements below, and I watch as her eyes cloud over in a lust-drunk haze.

She's losing sight of reality. Falling into my spell. Learning that her world begins and ends with *me*. It's in that moment that she falls apart, her shout of ecstasy throttled by my cock lodging itself in her throat.

There's a moment of sheer panic that crosses her features, but it's chased by the oblivion that follows, and her sweet cunt spasms uncontrollably around my tail.

Lesson. Fucking. Accomplished. The three words echo in my mind as I follow her into oblivion with a growl, my seed unloading into her with a force unlike any I've ever experienced.

She freezes, the sudden gush of my essence forcing its way into her.

"*Swallow*," I demand.

Her throat tries to comply, but it's too much. I've gone

too deep for her to properly contract, and I'm too lost to my rapture to pull back.

"*Fuck*, Viviana." It comes out rough. Harsh. *Furious*.

Her eyes are wild, her own pleasure still squeezing the shit out of my other appendage.

But she's going to truly choke if I don't pull back.

It takes serious effort. Effort that costs me a few precious moments of sensation. However, I force myself to release my grip on her hair to let her pull back. She does, going back on her knees and coughing as my cock leaves her mouth.

With a snarl, I fist her hair once more to yank her head back, then stroke myself and keep coming.

Her eyes are wide as I spill my seed all over her heaving breasts, my need to be inside her and on her overriding everything else.

This is my first time playing with a toy. And I nearly broke her.

It was always a risk. But watching her tits bounce tells me she's fine. That knowledge allows me to finish my release, my mind conjuring all the ways I intend to do this again. I won't push as deep next time. I'll… I'll pull back a little first. Warn her before I come. Something.

Because she *will* swallow my load. Every fucking drop.

I want her full of my essence, dripping with my seed, swollen from my ministrations, *tasting me on her tongue every moment of every day*.

Gods, just thinking about it has me spurting more onto her chest until she's saturated with my cum.

Her breaths are still coming in pants, her startled state a beautiful sight.

But it's not good enough.

I need more.

I pull my tail from her spasming pussy and free myself

from her hand, then guide the tip up to the mess I've made on her breasts. With a soft hum, I scoop a good portion of it onto the triangle end, then lift it to her parted lips.

I don't ask permission. I don't even speak. I simply push it inside—*where it fucking belongs*.

Her eyes blow wide, her nostrils flaring in response.

However, my good little pet doesn't question my intentions. She simply *swallows*. Then she takes it a step further by licking and sucking on my tail.

A pleased rumble leaves me, and I repeat the action by returning my tail to her tits and gathering more for her to devour.

She doesn't fight me, just continues to take my seed like a beautiful intended mate.

By the time she's finished, my dick is already throbbing and ready to fuck again.

Noticing it, her gaze turns wary.

And I grin. "You thought we were done?" I ask, gentling my tone to a taunting coo. "Oh, sweet little Viviana, I'm not human. It's going to take a lot more than a single orgasm to please me. So open your mouth. We're going to try this again. And we're not stopping until we get it right."

CHAPTER ELEVEN
VIVI

My throat is *raw*.

To the point that I can no longer swallow.

My legs are bruised from the shower tiles.

And I'm pretty sure I'm never going to be able to sit again, thanks to Ciprian's tail.

I've been on my knees for *hours*, taking his cock in my mouth, swallowing his cum, only to miss a few drops and having to start again.

He's determined to ensure he finishes entirely down my throat. But I can't take any more. And I don't know how to ask him to stop.

When he presses the head of his massive dick to my lips, I whimper. I can't help it. I've lost count of the number of orgasms exchanged between us. "*Ciprian*," I try to say, but it's a rasp of sound.

His grip in my hair tightens, and I know he's about to shove himself into my mouth for the sixth or seventh time. Only, he pulls my head back further, like he did what feels like hours ago when he came all over my breasts.

I try to meet his gaze, to tell him with my eyes that I need a break. Water. *Something.*

But the world starts to swim, and I can't focus on anything at all.

Darkness descends, only to blink back into bright color as my reality shifts. Chilling air hits me, drawing a hiss from my swollen lips. However, it's short-lived.

Something rumbles. Ciprian, I think. *Is he growling?*

"Drink," he murmurs, his voice very close to my ear.

I wince, unsure if I can *drink* any more of him right now. I'm so full of *him* that I don't think I'm capable of swallowing any more.

However, he doesn't give me a choice as he presses something hard and wet to my mouth. I feel like weeping as I part my lips to obey, to take another thrust, only all I receive is some warm liquid.

Is he jacking off into my mouth now? I wonder dizzily.

It's then that I realize my eyes are closed. I just don't have the energy to see anymore.

So I simply… swallow.

The taste isn't right. It's… it's sweeter than his cum. Thicker. Yet just as hot against my tongue.

My brow furrows as I try to determine what he's feeding me. Then I jump when I feel him touch my legs. "You're injured," he says, sounding annoyed. "I've hurt you."

No shit, I want to tell him. *That's what happens when you keep a woman on her knees for fucking hours.*

"Hmm," he hums. "Well, this is an interesting development. I suppose I should have expected it, though, with the blood exchange."

Blood exchange? I think, confused. *What blood exchange?*

"The one happening right now," he replies.

I mentally blink. *What? Is he talking to me or to someone else?*

"There is no one else I could be speaking to at present, pet," he murmurs. "Though, I should send a request down to Radu. I'll do that once I'm satisfied with your healing."

Okay… I'm entirely lost.

"You're not lost, Viviana. I merely brought you to my room so I can properly tend to you," he says. "I was too rough. Again. I'm sorry. Humans are just so… *fragile.*"

While I hear the latter part of what he's saying, I'm still focused on the former part because he responded to my thought. *You can read my mind?*

"I can now, yes," he says. "As I said, it's expected from the blood exchange."

Blood… exchange… I force my eyes open, needing to see *exactly* what I'm drinking. *Blood. I'm… you're feeding me… blood.*

"To heal you, yes." He stares down at me from above.

Because he's holding me.

In his lap.

And he's still wearing that pristine suit. He never once removed it, even while the water flowed freely behind me in the shower.

How many hours were you fucking my mouth? I want to demand.

"It was only ninety minutes or so," he tells me, clearly hearing the thought in my head. "Next time, we will aim for two hours."

I gape at him. *You're going to kill me.*

"Not purposely," he says, frowning a little. "In fact, I very much want to ensure you remain alive. That's why I'm feeding you my essence, Viviana." He pulls his wrist away from my mouth, his gaze going to my lips.

I merely gape at him as he leans down to lick me clean. Then gasp when his tongue slides in to meet my own.

One moment, he's forcing me suck his cock. Then he

gives me blood. And now… now he's kissing me with a sweetness that has my toes curling.

This is maddening, I think, bewildered. *I don't… I don't know how to do this.*

Neither do I, he whispers back into mind, his mental intrusion shocking me. *That's why we're going to learn together.*

How are you in my head? I ask, wary and startled. *Or have you always been able to do this?*

I've never been psychically connected to anyone before, Viviana. Only to you.

What does that mean?

Rather than respond, his hands move to my sides. Then he pulls me upright in his lap and forces me to straddle his thick thighs—all while continuing to kiss me.

It's like I'm a slave to his needs, my body moving with his in a submissive dance.

He deepens our embrace, his tongue mastering mine in languid strokes as his chest rumbles in approval. It's not a growl but a purr, and the sound lulls me into a strange sort of soothing trance.

I actually *sigh*.

Everything feels… safe. Calm. Utterly peaceful.

Which is a lie.

This monster just had me on my knees for… *only ninety minutes?* I think, bewildered. *God, it felt like hours…*

Maybe because it was a whirlwind of activity. I was just trying to keep up. Swallowing. Sucking. *Coming*.

I try to recount how many times he exploded in my mouth, but I can't. It's all a blur of sensuality and pleasure and… and *pain*.

Only, the pain is more recent. And it appears to be abating now. *Thanks to his blood*.

"Mmm," he hums against my mouth. "Your mind is… loud. Yet fascinating." He pulls back to stare at me, his irises crimson in color. "Having access to your thoughts will prove most useful during our next session, Viviana. I'll be able to better determine your limits."

"Or you could just ask me for my limits," I tell him, pleased that my throat appears to have magically recovered.

Magically… literally, I realize. *Because of his blood.*

But I ignore that part and focus on the monster I'm straddling.

"You could also give me a safe word," I inform him flatly. "But then, verbal consent doesn't seem to matter to you, does it?"

His eyebrow lifts. "You're displeased with me?"

"I'm more than displeased with you," I snarl at him. "I'm *furious* with you." Though, I can't really articulate *why*. I feel fine now.

But I didn't minutes ago.

I… I was well beyond my limits of *fine*.

I was terrified he might make me inhale his cum and *kill me*.

His lips curl down. "I stopped the moment your body told me to."

"That's not how this…" I trail off and close my eyes. "Ciprian. I realize you're a Strigoi King and used to having mistresses who will do whatever you want. Or…" Now it's my turn to frown.

Because he said he's never done this before, that he needed me to remain calm while he *learned* how to fuck my mouth.

Mine, specifically? Or… or in general?

"I'm so confused," I whisper, meaning it. "Is it that you've never been with a human before?" I guess out loud. "Is that what you meant?" I open my eyes once more and look at him. "You're used to other, er, Strigoi in bed?"

He stares at me. "I don't allow anyone in my bed, Viviana." He cants his head. "Sleep is a vulnerable state for a Strigoi."

"That's not what I meant."

A ghost of a smile tilts his lips on one side. "I know." He lifts his hand to my cheek, then runs the back of his fingers down my neck.

"Did you just make a joke…?" I ask slowly, trying to understand him.

"I don't joke." A serious statement. Yet I swear there's a glimmer of mirth in his gaze as his irises slowly return to an obsidian color. "I've never been with another being in an intimate manner, Viviana. You are my first. In all ways."

I gape at him. "*What?*" That can't be true. Or maybe we're having some sort of misunderstanding in terms. "You're several hundred years old."

"Over a thousand years, actually," he tells me.

"There's no way you're a virgin," I go on, almost ignoring his comment. But I mentally catalog the information since it's the first personal detail he's given me about himself.

Unless… unless he means it about being inexperienced.

"*Virgin* is a sweet term, one that feels too inadequate to describe who and what I am." He sits up a little straighter, his intense gaze holding mine. "As the Strigoi King, I need an heir. It's beneath me to indulge in a frivolous affair with an unworthy candidate. Therefore, I've waited for the right opportunity to… play."

His words roll through my head, my mind comprehending the concept behind them, but not quite believing what it means. "So you've never… been with a human."

"I've never been intimate with anyone," he says, repeating what he's already told me. "Except you." He cups my cheek again. "That's why it's important for you to remain still when I'm using you, pet. I'm learning the limits of our connection. And I do not wish to harm you."

"Using me." That phrase irritates me almost as much as it turns me on. "Using me for pleasure? Using me for an heir? Using me for… what exactly?"

"Yes."

I wait for him to elaborate.

He doesn't.

"That doesn't answer my question, Ciprian."

His jaw clenches. "Are you aware that it's improper for a pet to call a king by his first name? Some may even call it *rude*."

"Are you aware that it's rude to call a woman a pet?" I counter. "Are you aware that it's rude to tell a woman you want to use her? Or to fuck her mouth until she nearly passes out?" I glare at him. "It's also rude—"

His lips claim mine, silencing me.

I almost fall into the kiss. *Almost.*

Then I remember that he can apparently hear my thoughts.

So I continue listing ways he's been rude within my mind.

It's rude to use your tongue to silence someone.

It's rude to stick a tail in someone without asking.

It's rude to choke someone with your cock.

"Is it rude to gift your intended mate with so much pleasure that she passes out?" he asks, his lips brushing mine with every word. "Is it rude to feed her your blood so she survives and comes back stronger than ever?"

I glare at him. "It's rude to assume someone is your intended mate without actually asking." My words lack heat, mostly because my mind is whirring with the phrase *intended mate.*

What does that even mean? I wonder.

It means I intend to make you mine, he replies mentally. *It also means I would very much like you to stop chastising me now so I can properly care for you.*

Care for me how? I ask warily. *Because I don't think I can handle another orgasm right now, King Negru.* I purposely use his last name and title since he claimed it was *improper* for me to call him Ciprian.

"Mmm, I stand corrected," he says, brushing his nose against mine. "I like it when you call me by my first name."

"But it's *improper*, isn't it?" I sass back at him.

He smiles.

And I basically stop breathing.

Because *wow.*

He has a *beautiful* smile. It's unworldly handsome. Which, given that he's not of this world, makes sense. But it's really not fair for him to look that alluring.

"Your lack of fear where I'm concerned is truly thrilling," he says. "And borderline suicidal." He brushes his mouth against mine, then grabs my hips and lifts me off his lap. "I will feed you now."

I take several steps back, my knees shaking with the effort. He may have given me his blood, but I don't feel fully recovered yet. Or maybe… maybe it's panic making my legs shake. Regardless… "I'm not ready to eat more…" I trail off and look at his groin. "I…"

His lips curl again. "I'm sure I could entice you to change your mind. But I was referring to food. You can suck my cock for dessert."

"Lucky me," I deadpan.

He arches a brow. "You have no idea how lucky you

might become, Ms. Dalca. If you become my mate, you'll be the Strigoi Queen."

"And do I get a say in this potential future?" I demand. "Or is it assumed that I'll accept?"

His gaze runs over me as he stands. "You're displeased with me."

"No shit," I snap. "You just treated me like a sex doll, *Your Highness*." I can't help the note of sarcasm in my tone. "I realize you're a Strigoi, but I'm a human. I have to be able to breathe."

"I believe I ensured you inhaled just fine through the experience." He steps around me and starts to walk away, dismissing the conversation.

"Don't do that," I tell him. "Don't treat me like I'm insignificant."

He pauses and turns, his brow furrowed. "In what way have I done this?"

"You never let me finish talking."

"Because your commentary is frivolous."

"Not to me," I reply, suddenly exhausted. "It's not *frivolous* to me."

"I see." He turns again, and my shoulders fall.

Defeat washes over me.

This is pointless, I think. *He's not human.*

I'm not, he replies into my mind. *But I know you need sustenance, so I shall have something brought up. We will talk more in a few minutes.*

CHAPTER TWELVE
CIPRIAN

VIVIANA'S EMOTIONS and thoughts warm my mind as I enter the sitting area just off of my suite.

Pressing a button on a nearby tablet, I say, "Radu?"

"Yes, my lord?"

"Could you please arrange a late lunch for me and Ms. Dalca to enjoy in my rooms?"

"Of course, my lord. Any meal preferences?"

"No broccoli" is all I can reply, but as I sense Viviana joining me, I turn to face her. "Are you craving anything in particular?"

She stares at me. "Something warm for my throat might be nice."

I arch a brow, wondering if she's being purposely coquettish or if she means it. "Soup, perhaps?"

Something in her gaze lights up. "Tomato soup?"

It's a strange choice, but I repeat it to Radu.

"I'm certain our chef could make something that suits, my lord," he promises me. "Would Ms. Dalca like anything to go with it? A grilled cheese, perhaps?"

I'm about to comment on that bizarre choice when my

intended mate smiles and nods. So I simply say, "Yes, I believe she would enjoy that." *Though, I have no idea why,* I think.

Because it's amazing, she fires back into my mind.

And I'm rather pleased to hear that instant response, as she appeared a little… out of sorts when I left the bedroom.

"Any cheese preferences?" Radu asks, and since he doesn't use my title, I assume he's talking to Viviana. So I arch a brow at her, daring her to answer.

"Anything French would be nice," she replies.

"Of course, Ms. Dalca," he murmurs, a hint of warmth in his tone. "Any other requests?"

"Dessert," she says, giving me a look. "Something chocolaty and *not* salty."

My eyebrows lift.

But Radu can't see me as he eagerly murmurs, "I know exactly what to prepare. We'll be up soon."

The line goes dead, his formalities in addressing me seeming to have disappeared. If I didn't like the human male so much, I might be tempted to castigate him later for it.

However, I'm far more intrigued by my pet very clearly saying she will not be having my cock for dessert. "Would you prefer to suck me off as an appetizer, pet?"

"No." It's a flat answer, one I don't particularly care for.

"You're rejecting me?"

"No," she repeats. "I'm establishing a boundary. I want a safe word."

"What is the meaning or purpose of a safe word?"

"It gives me some control in intimate encounters and allows me to tell you when you've gone too far."

"And if I disagree with the assessment?" I question. "If I feel you're using the word inappropriately?"

"That's not the point, Your Highness." She folds her arms, drawing my gaze to her bare breasts. "The word is for *me* so that *I* can voice when something makes me uncomfortable. And if you want to be a good intimacy partner, you will respect my choice to use it."

"I believe we already established that we're not equals here."

"More than established, yes," she replies, sounding tired again. "Do you care if I feel safe, my king?"

"Stop using titles and call me Ciprian."

"You pointed out that it's rude."

"Because it is," I inform her. "It goes against the customs of my kind. Only one person ever refers to me as Ciprian, and it's my best friend. And only ever when we're alone." I start toward her, wanting to touch her. "I would like for you to call me Ciprian, too. Also… when we're alone."

"And when we're not?" she asks, her wary tone not lost on me.

"For now, if we are around others, you will need to address me by my title. Otherwise, my fellow Strigoi may take offense. That's why rules are important. Formalities, too."

"If you're the king, don't you make the rules?"

"Some," I admit. "But not all. And you're a human. Your kind is inferior to mine."

"Yet you've referred to me as your *intended mate*," she says. "How does that work?"

"It works quite well, I assure you," I murmur, cupping her jaw and drawing her gaze up to mine. "Strigoi often take humans as mates, Viviana."

"So your kind enjoys submissive partners?"

I shrug. "Many of us do, yes. But not all of my kind."

"I was being sarcastic." Her exhaustion is palpable again, as is her mounting agitation.

"Explain it to me," I ask her. "Tell me what you mean, Viviana. Help me understand. Please."

It's the softest I've ever spoken to anyone in my entire existence.

However, this female has gifted me with a pleasure unlike anything I've ever known. And not just physically. Her fiery nature pleases me. It probably shouldn't. But I like that she doesn't fear me. It's enthralling. It makes me feel… *human.*

Which is bizarre.

I'm used to invoking terror unless using the art of compulsion.

Yet Viviana studies me with interest in her gaze. Lust. *Excitement.*

Although, right now, she's looking at me like she's thinking about stabbing me. And that only intrigues me more.

"Humans are beneath your kind," she says. "Right?"

"Mortals are not as strong or as powerful as Strigoi, yes."

"Yet Strigoi take humans as mates, thus suggesting that your kind enjoys having an inferior partner in a relationship. Some might call that a submissive." She bristles a little. "But even a submissive is allowed a safe word. So I suppose a slave is more accurate. Which gives credence to you calling me a pet, I guess."

My gaze narrows a bit, understanding creeping in. "You're offended."

"I'm a lot of things right now, Your Highness," she mutters, closing her eyes as she rubs the goose bumps pebbling along her arms. "This has been an overwhelming… God, has it only been twenty-four hours since I arrived here?"

"Yes. But time is a mortal construct. And our history already spans years, Viviana, making it the longest courtship of my existence."

She blinks. "Courtship? You think this is a *courtship*?"

"Yes," I repeat, then pull her into my arms and lift her into the air.

She squeals in response, her mind shouting alarm at the things she assumes I'm about to do to her.

"Relax, Ms. Dalca," I tell her. "I'm simply carrying you into my closet to find something for you to wear so that you'll stop shivering."

The tension doesn't leave her form, not even as I set her down to search for a shirt.

Once I find a suitably soft fabric, I unbutton it and drape it around her petite shoulders. The length hits her thighs, making it resemble a dress on her. One I rather like since it's my shirt and her wearing it makes her look like she belongs to me.

She says nothing as I fasten the buttons up her torso, just watches me with distrust in her gaze.

"In my home world, humans are aware that Strigoi exist. We've formed a society together, one where Strigoi protect the mortals and mortals feed the Strigoi. So while yes, humans are seen as inferior due to their weaker states, they're not treated as *slaves*."

I thread my fingers through hers and lead her from the closest but head into the bathroom rather than back into the bedroom.

Pausing at a set of drawers, I find a comb, then turn her to face the mirror while I begin to gently detangle her hair. It's the least I can do since the dark strands are knotted from my ministrations.

Though, I may need to have her shower again, as I'm rather certain some of this is from my seed, not just my fingers fisting her thick hair.

However, rather than comment on that, I continue telling her about the Strigoi Kingdom and the relationships between my kind and humans.

"Strigoi often take mortals as lovers and mates because our kinds rely on the other to survive. The heart of the relationship is a blood exchange—Strigoi need mortal essences to stay alive, and humans can achieve true immortality by imbibing from a Strigoi's vein."

"I-immortality?" she stammers, meeting my gaze in the mirror. "Drinking from you makes me immortal?"

"It can, yes. If you imbibe enough." I find a particularly difficult knot and focus on it for a long moment, all while she watches me.

After the comb successfully goes through the cluster of strands, I continue explaining the mate-bond between Strigoi and humans. I tell her how it takes three blood exchanges to fully ignite, but a vow and sex to marry the souls together.

"Strigoi mate for life," I inform her quietly. "Once we choose our other half, we don't feed from anyone else. We don't fuck anyone else, either." I tell her that part while holding her gaze again. "Strigoi are *very* possessive creatures, Ms. Dalca. We're loyal, too. And our blood connections are sacred."

She swallows, drawing my gaze down to her slender throat. I very much enjoyed how that felt around my cock. But I don't tell her that now. I've upset her—something that's far more evident to me now that I can hear her thoughts—and I want to fix it.

"As I told you, I'm new to this. No other human has tempted me like you do. It's…" I trail off, searching for the right words to help her understand. "I feel overwhelmed with lust, Viviana. All I want to do is live inside you. To experience pleasure. To finally feel connected to another being."

I finish combing her hair, letting my explanation settle between us.

Her mind seems to be processing the statements, her anger somewhat abating. However, I can tell the matter of verbal consent still bothers her.

So while she considers everything I said, I consider everything she's said. Particularly about her desire to have a *safe word*. It's an interesting concept regarding control, one I'm intrigued by.

"If you voice your word of choice, and I do not agree with the timing and don't stop, that harms trust between us, yes?" I ask, wanting to be sure I understand the purpose of her needing this boundary.

"Yes," she answers without hesitation. "If you ignore it, that defeats the purpose."

"And will make you distrust me."

"Absolutely." Her eyes find mine in the mirror again. "And I already don't trust you not to hurt me."

Irritation prickles my chest. Irritation… at myself. Because I don't particularly care for her distrust. "I've hurt you?"

"You've scared me," she clarifies. "A lot."

I frown. "You don't seem to fear me."

"I don't fear what you are, King Negru. But I'm terrified of what you might do to me—on purpose or not."

It's on the tip of my tongue to repeat my request to be called *Ciprian*. However, hearing the reason for it in her head forces me not to voice it.

The heart of our ensuing issue is trust.

She's using my title to maintain a formality, a distance, to keep this conversation from becoming intimate.

Because she does not feel safe with me.

"I understand now, thank you," I murmur, pleased that she's provided me with guidance. This is probably the longest conversation I've had with a person who isn't Marius. And I find that I'm also satisfied with that realization.

Reaching around her, I set the comb down, then rest my palms on the counter, caging her between my body and the sink before us.

"What would you like your safe word to be, Ms. Dalca?" I ask against her ear while holding her gaze in the mirror.

Her heart rate escalates. "Why? Are you going to make me kneel again?"

"Absolutely, yes," I inform her softly, then kiss her thundering pulse. "I enjoyed your mouth, Viviana."

"I'm n-not ready," she stammers, her body tensing against mine.

Which has me frowning once more. "Not ready to provide your safe word? Or not ready to kneel?"

"Both," she whispers, and her scent changes. "I need some time to recover. Please. I don't want to suck your cock right now."

"Hmm." I kiss her neck, then nuzzle her throat. "Does that mean you would likely use your safe word on me if I attempted to feed you my cock right now?"

"Yes." There isn't a hint of hesitation. In fact, it comes out a little defiant. Angry. And her mind helps me understand why. *Not that I expect you to acknowledge it or accept it*, she's thinking.

Hmm. My intended mate fully expects me to disregard her desires and fulfill my own instead.

Because that's what I've shown her through my actions.

She seems to be oblivious to the fact that I've also been taking care of her—stopping when I knew she couldn't take any more, healing her with my blood, and helping to groom her just moments ago.

I nod and brush my lips against her temple. Rather than speak, I thread my fingers through hers and pull her with me as we leave the bathroom to head through my bedroom to the sitting area once more.

Her steps are tense, her body even tenser.

Nothing I say will help ease her from this mental torment, so I decide to demonstrate intent through action.

Without speaking, I turn and grab her hips, then lift her to sit in my favorite chair.

Leaving her, I go to the bar to pour two glasses of red wine. However, as I return, I realize I should have asked her for a preference. So I set them down on the end table, then look at her. "Do you like wine?"

She glances at me and then at the crimson liquid. "I… I would prefer not to drink alcohol right now."

I crouch down so that we're at eye level with one another. "Tell me what you would prefer, please."

She studies me. "Is this where you instruct me to unzip your pants and drink from your cock?"

"Only if that's what you desire to imbibe," I say, striving for patience. "But you just told me you're not interested in sucking my cock at the moment. So what would you like, Ms Dalca?"

Her gaze runs over me. "You're confusing me."

"It's not intentional."

"I've gathered that." She tucks her knees up and wraps her arms around them. "Can I be honest?"

"I would prefer that, yes," I tell her.

"Then I would really love a cup of coffee right now. Or a jug of it."

My eyebrow lifts. "A jug of coffee?"

"A pot," she corrects. "Or… or a really large cup. With hazelnut cream."

I stare at her for a beat, then straighten and go to call Radu again. He hesitates a little on the hazelnut part but says he'll make it happen. I trust him to handle it, grab a bottle of water from my bar fridge, and take it over to Viviana.

Her eyes are wide when I take over the chair beside her. "I've shocked you." It's not a question but a statement; I can hear the startled alarm in her mind. "I'm not cruel, Ms. Dalca. If you need something, voice it, and I will do what I can to appease you."

She says nothing for a long moment but eventually opens the water I set beside her and presses it to her lips. I observe her throat as it works, once again thinking about how it felt to fuck her mouth.

I'm hard. But I'm rather certain I'm going to exist in this state indefinitely now that I've found a potential mate.

Or rather, my *intended* mate.

There's nothing *potential* about her anymore. She's not a toy. But she is my pet. Only, I don't view that term as negatively as she seems to.

"Calling you *pet* isn't meant to be rude," I say, recounting her earlier statement to the contrary. "I mean it affectionately, as in I want to care for you and your needs." I pick up one of the glasses of wine and swirl it in the glass.

I'm about to ask if she prefers *princess* or another endearment when I sense Marius's approach.

My spine stiffens, my gaze narrowing at the door.

I dismissed him earlier after Viviana refused to leave. *So why is he still here?*

His knuckles rap against the wood, then he pushes through without an invitation. "Radu has run out to find hazelnut cream for your guest," he announces as he enters with a tray balanced on one hand. "I offered to bring up your late lunch."

By *offered*, I assume he means he took the tray from one of Radu's staff members and flew it up here without comment.

Which means my best friend is up to something. "Can I help you, Marius?"

"No," he says, setting the tray down on the rectangular table situated in the middle of my seating room. "I'm here to help you, though."

"Of course you are," I deadpan.

He smiles and collapses on the couch across from me, then looks at Viviana. She's still curled up in my favorite chair with her legs tucked upward. "You look famished, darling. You should eat." He leans forward. "Would you like me to feed you?"

"Touch her and I will end you," I growl, not bothering to mask the fury underlining my threat.

His smile only intensifies. "You have no idea how thrilled I am by this development."

My jaw tightens. "You can go now, Marius."

"But you should know, I'm keeping the guest wing," he goes on, ignoring me. "It's already been renamed as mine. Consider it payment for running the kingdom in your absence."

I nearly roll my eyes. "I've been ruling. You've been delivering."

He kicks his feet up on the table beside the tray and crosses his ankles. "Semantics."

"Semantics that mean something," I point out. "You act as though you'll be relinquishing a hardship. Won't you miss your harem?"

"Oh, I fully intend to keep them in my wing," he says, winking at Viviana. "You're welcome to visit, too, darling."

"Are you trying to get yourself killed?" I ask him seriously. "Best friend or not, I will rip your heart out and feed it to you."

His mirth is palpable. "She's been here a day and already has your balls in a vise. I love it."

"Fuck off, Marius."

"No." His feet drop to the floor, and he leans forward to uncover the tray. "I'm joining you both for lunch so we can discuss your return to the Strigoi Kingdom. And the presentation of your intended mate."

CHAPTER THIRTEEN
VIVI

My head is spinning.

However, despite the conversation, all I can really focus on is the grilled cheese melt a few feet away from me. I'm *starving*. I didn't realize that until the scent hit me, but now it's all I can think about.

"Unless you plan to breed her first?" Marius asks, his words momentarily returning my attention to him. "I mean, that's one way to guarantee her acceptance among our kind. They can't deny a woman impregnated with a royal heir, yeah?"

"Stop speaking, Marius," Ciprian says.

"You're going to *breed* me?" I blurt out, feeling even dizzier now.

Too much information has been exchanged. Too many demands made. Too much *insanity*.

In all my wildest dreams of coming here, of finding *him*, never could I have imagined everything that's transpired. And in such a short amount of time, too.

"Leave, Marius." The demand echoes through the room, causing me to want to shrink back against the chair.

It's all too much.

I'm exhausted. I'm hungry. I'm *wrecked.*

And now he wants to breed me?

He's a one-thousand-year-old virgin Strigoi. A monster who has waited for an ideal mate. A male… who clearly desires me when he's apparently never desired another.

It's intimidating. Overwhelming. *Intoxicating.*

But impregnating me?

I'm in no way ready for that, I think. *God, I don't even know if he can fit inside me. He barely fit in my mouth!*

I bury my head in my knees, trying desperately to control my raging emotions. This isn't me at all. I never respond this way.

I'm the human who sought out a creature of the night. The woman who traveled for half a day on a plane to reach a foreign country and hunt down a vampire.

And now I'm curled in on myself like a broken doll.

All because of the intense madness swimming around me.

The way Ciprian used me in the shower… hurt my confidence. Maybe it's because I couldn't keep up with him? Or it was just too much sensation? I'm not sure. But it infuriated me afterward. Then he started talking, telling me how he's never been with anyone before, and I… I *felt* something.

Something frightening.

Something immense.

Something… *life-changing.*

I went from feeling used to feeling *special.* Because this monster chose me. After over a thousand years of life, he decided *I* was worthy of his lust.

Which is asinine.

I shouldn't feel *special* because a millennium-old virgin decided he wanted me.

Yet, I couldn't stop the flutters from igniting in my belly or the pitter-patter of my heart.

He made me feel cherished in an utterly bizarre way. Like I may be someone worthy of more.

And now his familiar… or whatever Marius is to him… is talking about Ciprian *breeding* me.

The notion should mortify me. It sort of does, I guess, but not in the right way. Because my mortification is born from the realization that I wouldn't mind being fucked by Ciprian Negru.

In fact, just the concept of it sends cascades of warmth through my veins.

I've lost my mind.

Or, more likely, I'm under some sort of enchantment. A spell woven by the Strigoi King. A mating incantation, perhaps?

"Viviana." Ciprian's voice is deep, hypnotic, and powerful. It's also extremely close, which has me blinking in confusion.

He's kneeling in front of me, his hands on my face.

How long has he been like this? I wonder, searching his stoic expression. *How long has he been saying my name?*

"A few minutes," he replies, clearly still able to read my mind.

Is it permanent? I swallow. *Is this mental connection… a forever kind of thing?*

"Yes, and it'll only deepen if we finalize our mating," he tells me, his thumb drawing along my lower lip. "You need to eat, *regina mea*."

I blink again, those two foreign words repeating in my head. *What does that mean?*

"*My queen*." He leans in to brush a kiss against my mouth. "Here." He moves, then hands me a plate with the grilled cheese on it. "The soup is still too hot. When it's ready, I'll feed it to you."

An image of him using his tail pops into my head, making me shiver. In an effort to ignore the mental depiction, I pick up the sandwich and shove it into my mouth.

However, he must have overheard my thoughts. Or… or maybe he saw it somehow? Because the appendage in question creeps up my leg as he softly questions, "You wish to burn my tail?"

I choke on the cheese and bread, causing him to grab my water and push it toward me. I take it from him and wince as I force the food down my throat.

He observes, his black irises flickering with crimson flares. But his lips are curled down in a frown, something I've gathered isn't typical for him. Just like his smiles.

This male seems to be quite unfamiliar with emotions.

I'm not sure if it's my connection to his mind telling me that, or instincts, or something else entirely. And I'm too exhausted to try to determine the source of my knowledge. I just know that he's experiencing a lot of firsts right now.

Including his feelings toward me.

"Is your desire born of a need to punish me?" he goes on.

And if I were still eating, I would be choking again.

"Because my tail is quite sensitive. Dipping it into the soup would be… uncomfortable. But if it's your wish—"

I press my finger to his lips, needing him to stop. "My mind isn't a reliable narrator right now, Your Highness."

His brow furrows even more.

"What I mean is, my thoughts are compromised. I'm… I'm not feeling like myself. A lot has happened, and I'm struggling to comprehend it all. Which means my brain is a little frazzled and therefore… unreliable. So if you overhear something, don't overthink it. I'm just processing. Sort of."

Well, that was a mouthful of gibberish.

But his forehead is less crinkled now, so he seems to somewhat understand what I've said.

Just to ensure we're on the same page, I add, "So, no, I don't want to burn your tail. When you said you were going to feed me, I thought of how you fed me earlier." My cheeks heat with the words, and I clear my throat. "I just… I just want a spoon. Please. Food. Eat. You know? Anyway." I shake my head, aware that I sound like a lunatic. "Ignore me."

"No."

I startle. "What?"

"I refuse to *ignore* you." He nods at my plate. "Now eat."

"It's…" I trail off, deciding that explaining what I meant by *ignore me* isn't worth the energy. I'll just… do what he demanded and enjoy my grilled cheese.

Because it's *really* good. Like, easily the best one I've ever tasted. Whatever French cheeses his chef used are amazing.

When I'm about halfway done, a spoon appears, and I realize that Ciprian is attempting to feed me the soup. "It's an appropriate temperature now."

I almost make a joke to ask if he tested it with his tail, but I refrain and simply open my mouth instead.

His gaze locks on my lips as he feeds me, his cheekbones seeming to become more pronounced from him clenching his jaw.

I swallow, which appears to make it worse, because his eyes narrow.

However, he brings another bite up for me to consume.

So I do. And we continue the dance for several minutes before finally, I grab his wrist and say, "The way you're looking at me is starting to make me feel like food."

"You are food," he murmurs. "*For me.*"

I shiver. "Does that mean you plan to bite me?"

"Many times, yes. For eternity, I hope." He pushes forward with the spoon, slipping it between my lips and watching as I swallow. "But you will give me a safe word first, something to say if I take too much or push too far. I do not wish to upset you again."

"You didn't…" I trail off.

I was about to say he didn't upset me, which isn't true. He infuriated me.

However, his explanations have helped me understand why he pushed me the way he did. And he does seem to be trying to talk to me now instead of merely using me for pleasure.

That doesn't mean I feel safe, though.

Which is… strangely arousing. I shouldn't like the way he's staring at me right now—like I'm prey—but I do.

And since he can hear my thoughts, he knows it, too.

"Why can't I read your mind?" I blurt out, wishing I knew what he was thinking right now. "I only hear you when you talk in my head."

He straightens—and I realize he's still kneeling in front of me, yet he's so big that we're eye level—and sets the bowl down on the table. "When we're fully mated, you will have unfettered access to my every thought."

"When?" I echo.

"When," he repeats sternly. "You just need to pass the trials. Then you can be mine."

"Trials?" I feel like we're just reiterating words back and forth. But this one feels like a very important one to clarify. "What *trials*?"

"There are certain expectations of a Strigoi King's mate, expectations that my kind will require you to meet." He brushes his knuckles along my cheek. "Fearlessness is one of them. A willingness to breed is another. And loyalty is paramount."

With those profound statements, he stands and turns toward the door just as someone knocks.

"Enter," he calls.

A shorter man with silver-black hair walks in holding a tray. "My lord," he greets. "I ended up making the hazelnut creamer from scratch, as it was faster than driving into town. If our guest dislikes it, I will go shopping."

Ciprian looks at me. "Is this acceptable to you, Ms. Dalca?"

My lashes flutter. "That he attempted to make hazelnut cream… from scratch?" I ask slowly. "No. If I had known he would go through all that trouble, I would have just asked for some milk and sugar." I look at the elderly male. "Please don't feel the need to do something that extravagant for me. I don't want to cause issues for the kitchen."

The older man smiles, a pair of dimples appearing on his cheeks.

He's really quite handsome for his age.

I imagine thirty or forty years ago, he acquired a lot of feminine attention.

Masculine attention, too, Ciprian says flatly into my mind. *Radu prefers men.* He faces me fully, his dark eyes grabbing and holding mine. *I also happen to care for him a great deal. So if you could stop thinking about his attractiveness, that would be kind, as I do not fancy the notion of killing him. And yet, my inner beast is currently demanding his slaughter.*

I blink, startled. *Sorry. I'm not sexually attracted to him, King Negru. Just… noting that he's attractive.*

The distinction does not appeal to my beast.

Then remind your beast that I sucked your cock several times today. So he owes me some grace, I snap back at him.

Ciprian arches a brow. *You're making me think about dessert, regina mea.*

How nice for you. I'll be enjoying my coffee. I finally look at the elderly man again—the one I now know is Radu—and smile. "Thank you for bringing this up for me and for making the cream. I'm sure it's divine."

I swear I hear Ciprian growl in my head.

"Do you mind setting it on the table over there?" I ask, gesturing with my chin toward a small dining table near the bar area. It seems like a safer choice than asking him to set it down next to the simmering Strigoi King.

"Of course, my lady," he murmurs, walking over to where the two chairs are tucked into a tall wooden table. "Would either of you care for anything else?"

"No," Ciprian says before I can reply. "We're fine."

"Thank you, Radu," I add, mostly to be polite. And also to piss off Ciprian a little bit more. *If you hurt this nice man, I will never suck your cock again,* I tell my Strigoi King. *I'll bite you instead.*

His wings whoosh as he spins toward me. *Biting is foreplay to a Strigoi, regina mea.*

Not the way I intend it, I promise him, looking up to meet his gaze. *Now be nice and stop growling in my head.*

He narrows his eyes as the door closes to his suite. "You have much to learn about a Strigoi's possessive instincts."

"It seems I have a lot to learn in general," I counter, finally feeling more like myself. "Now I'm going to go pour myself a cup of coffee, and then you're going to tell me more about the trials."

"Or I'll simply bend you over the table and fuck you instead," he says.

I give him the sweetest smile I can muster and reply, "If you do that in my current mood, I'll refuse to come for you." I step into his space and press my palm to his chest. "And trust me, Ciprian, you want me to climax while your cock is deep inside me. It'll give you the best pleasure of your life. Just ask your tail."

With that, I push him a step backward, then walk around him to go grab a cup of coffee.

The growls in my head intensify.

Which causes my heart to race in response.

I'm playing with fire. I know I am. But this Strigoi has me all messed up in the head. I may as well return the favor.

CHAPTER FOURTEEN
CIPRIAN

I FIND Marius waiting for me in my study several hours after Viviana finished her coffee. His smug expression makes me want to spar.

Or maybe that's a result of the beast raging within me.

I've spent the last five hours of my life… *talking*.

I can't remember a time I've ever spoken this much, and I don't fancy speaking more now.

But it seems my best friend has other ideas.

"Shouldn't you be in the Strigoi Kingdom with your harem?" I demand.

"Shouldn't you be in a rut in your chambers with your delicious intended?" he counters.

My wings flare out from my back, my chest rumbling with a snarl. "If you're looking for a fight, Marius, you've come to the right place."

"If that's what it takes, so be it." He pushes off the chair, his own wings bursting to life and shredding his tailored shirt in the process. "On the ground or in the air?"

I stare at him. "If that's what it takes?" I echo at him. "What the fuck does that even mean?"

"It means someone has to push you." He utters the words clearly. Efficiently. *Truthfully.* "You've finally found a worthy candidate. The Strigoi are eager to meet her."

His words are not ones I expected to hear. "You've told them about Viviana? Before I was ready to announce her?"

"I didn't have to. Your energy traverses the realms, Ciprian." He takes a step back and draws his fingers through his long blond hair. "You're the Strigoi King. It doesn't matter where you are—we all *feel* you. And the moment you learned of Viviana Dalca's existence, we sensed your intrigue, too."

I stare at him. "What?"

"I had hoped that the moment you met the human in person, you would recognize her as yours and immediately present her before the kingdom for testing. Instead, you decided to play. Given your eternity of celibacy, I understood. But the Strigoi are growing impatient."

"And you've chosen to wait until now to share all of this information with me?" I demand.

"Yes." His amusement is no longer prominent, the warrior I befriended ages ago now peering at me through narrowed blue eyes.

"Why?"

"Because it's my duty as your second-in-command to be the first one to evaluate your chosen candidate," he tells me, his words underlined with a dominance he rarely exudes in my presence. "That's the initial trial, Ciprian, the one that starts the process. And she passed."

I continue studying him. "You're telling me her trials have already begun."

"Yes."

"But she hasn't consented to be my mate yet."

He arches a brow. "You suddenly care about her consent?"

My teeth grind together as I begin to pace. Twenty-four hours ago, I would have questioned my own sanity in this conversation.

However, that was before gaining access to her mind.

"She's complicated," I mutter. "She… she makes me consider things in a new light."

A chuckle escapes Marius, some of his natural humor seeming to return. "That's fascinating."

"Fuck off."

"No." He steps into my path. "You need to take her home for the next trial, Ciprian."

"She's not ready."

"Doesn't matter."

"It does," I argue. "If she's meant to be my queen, then her wishes will be respected not just by me but also by our kind."

His jaw flexes, his irritation palpable. "Give me a timeline."

I arch a brow. "You're making demands of me now?"

"On behalf of the Strigoi, yes, Ciprian, I am. Your intended must participate in the trials. You know what will happen if she doesn't."

"I haven't even presented her yet."

"Not to the kingdom, no. But you did to me. And as I already stated—"

"You were the first trial," I interject, growling in irritation. "You could have fucking warned me, Marius."

"You should have fucking expected it," he counters. "Why do you think I so dutifully agreed to retrieve her for you?"

"Because you're a good friend."

"The best," he tells me. "Which is why I would have killed her without hesitation if—"

I have him up against the wall in a blink, my beast furious at even the notion of what he would have or could have done to my intended. "I trusted you with her *life*."

"Yes," he chokes out, his hand on my wrist as I close my palm around his throat.

His wings beat against the wall, his expression hardening.

"It's… my *duty*… to protect… you, Ci…" He's out of oxygen and can't finish his statement.

But I don't need him to.

The words *duty* and *protect* grate on my nerves.

Because he's right.

Fuck, he's right about *everything*.

He's right that I should have anticipated this. Known that he would be the first trial. Understood that the Strigoi would feel my intentions. Been aware of what would happen next. Expected that he would kill her if he found her unworthy, if only to spare me from the pain of failure.

And fuck. He's right about me losing myself to my lust upon her arrival, too.

"She's infuriatingly tempting," I mutter, releasing him and taking a step back. "You would have me present her as a potential queen before I've fully tasted her myself." The notion exasperates me. Mostly because I don't want to share her with anyone, let alone all of my kind. "She's mine. I want her first."

It's… it's not about sex.

I won't have to share her in *that* way.

But I will have to let the Strigoi know her. See her. Talk to her. Consume her time. Befriend her. *Test her…*

"Viviana doesn't trust me, Marius. I want to fix that

before I allow her to continue in the trials. She needs to feel safe. Otherwise…"

"You're worried she won't survive," he says, his voice already normal again, like I didn't nearly crush his windpipe moments ago.

"Yes." I face him. "I need more time."

"How much more?" he asks.

"A month?" I suggest.

He huffs a laugh. "No. You know that's impossible."

I do, but it felt appropriate to try. "A week, then."

"Seven days," he murmurs, his gaze turning thoughtful. "I can take that request back to the Strigoi."

"Thank you."

"Don't thank me yet," he says, sounding serious again. "The longer you keep her from our kind, the harsher her trials will become, Ciprian. The Strigoi are impatient to meet their potential queen, and while it may not be Viviana's fault that it's taken this long for her to appear, they blame her nonetheless."

I drag my fingers through my hair, hating what he's pointing out. "It's my failure, not hers."

"It's not a failure at all. You've been testing her in your own way since learning of her existence, seeing how far she would push to find you. I would argue that without those years of preparation, she may not have been ready for you. But she is now. You just have to… push her a little more."

"If I push more, she'll retreat." I could hear it in her mind.

I've discovered a limit.

"She needs to feel safe." Which means I have to find a balance between prodding her boundaries and ensuring I don't go too far.

"Where is she now? Back in her cage?"

I give him a flat look. "No. I left her napping in my bed."

The absolute delight that crosses his features has me nearly rolling my eyes again.

"You should go wake her up in a creative way," he suggests. "Afterward, you can inform her that the trials have begun."

Now I do roll my eyes. "Fairly certain me touching her is the opposite of safe. In her mind, anyway." A fact that grates on my nerves because I haven't truly harmed her. I've made sure of it. But she doesn't trust me not to hurt her, which is precisely the problem.

"Prove otherwise." He gives me a smile. "Focus on her pleasure, not your own. You'll be amazed by what she begs for next."

"I don't need a tutorial on females, Marius."

"Says the ancient virgin," he drawls. "Use your mouth, but not your teeth. And make sure you play with her clit. Women like that."

I take a step toward him, and he jumps back with his hands in the air. "I'm leaving."

"Good," I growl. "And don't ever talk about my mate's pussy again. Don't even think about her that way. She's *mine*, Marius."

"Your *intended*, not your *mate*," he corrects me. Then he runs for the portal mirror because he knows I'm seconds from punching him in the face. "Seven days, Ciprian."

He practically leaps through the glass before I can comment.

"Coward," I mutter, my wings rustling at my back as my tail whips around behind me.

I don't need an anatomy lesson or a reminder that Viviana isn't my mate yet.

I know what a fucking clit is, too. I had one in my mouth last night. Though, I did use my teeth.

"Focus on her pleasure," I echo. "I have. Several times."

But I also enjoyed myself, too. That's why I made her come initially—because I wanted to watch her fall apart.

How am I supposed to solely concentrate on her when I like observing her climax? I wonder. I'll always get something out of it. She's fucking stunning when she's lost to the throes of passion. I can't indulge in the experience without some personal satisfaction.

Which makes his advice ridiculous.

Growling, I start to pace my office. I came in here to do some reading. Now all I want to do is return to my female.

She's asleep in my bed.

I should guard her. Keep her safe by being nearby. Perhaps that will make her feel better?

"*Fuck.*" This was much easier when I didn't have access to her mind. I didn't consider the consequences of giving her blood, just fed her my essence to help heal her throat.

A throat I used too roughly, thereby requiring my aid in her recovery. Yet another consequence I didn't consider while lost to my beast's needs.

All of this is my fault.

And I despise that fact.

I'm renowned for my control. However, Viviana is challenging my basic principles. She's confusing my instincts, making me yearn for her even more than I already did.

It's maddening.

And confounding.

I'm the superior. The Strigoi King. Yet this female has brought me to my knees both figuratively and literally.

Another growl escapes me as I leave my office, my

intention to read no longer viable. I can't be away from her. I just… I just want to watch her. Hold her. *Fuck her*.

My teeth grind together, my dick hardening with the thought.

She's mine. My intended. My queen. My pet. She may not like that endearment, but it doesn't change how I feel about her. She's mine to care for. Mine to please. *Mine to possess*.

I just need to figure out how to help her understand that I won't irrevocably harm her. I'm larger. My stamina is… intense. But I listened to her body earlier. I stopped when I sensed her physical limit. What I didn't account for was her mental one.

Which, I suppose, is where the safe word comes into play.

Hmm. I enter the foyer—my office is on the first floor—and fly up to the second-floor landing to head toward my suite.

I have a tablet in there that I can use to read more about her request. I should have done that instead of venturing into my office, but I thought some space would allow me to regain control of my raging need.

I was wrong.

My craving for her has only increased in the short time I've been away.

Her scent hits me as I enter my rooms, my beast instantly quieting inside as my hunter instincts are engaged. *Our prey is in the bed. And she's aroused.*

Fuck.

That spiced citrus aroma has my dick aching in a heartbeat. I'm going to have to find some way to relieve myself. Some way to calm this tumultuous urge to *claim*.

I want to live inside her for eternity. Feel her cunt milk

my cock. Fill her with my seed. Demand that she live on my cum alone.

Gods, I'm utterly fucked.

If the Strigoi don't allow me to take this female as mine, I will lose my sanity. She is my present and my future. There will be no discussions. No denials. *No failure.*

Which means I have seven days to prepare her.

Seven days to indulge in her flesh.

Seven days to make her understand what it means to be a Strigoi King's mate.

Our lessons will begin now, I decide, stalking toward my bedchamber to where she's twisted in the sheets. She's lost to sleep. And she's *moaning.*

Every part of me stills, my gaze on her sweet form.

She's dreaming.

"Ciprian," she whispers, her eyes closed as her hips gyrate.

Fuck. She's not just dreaming… she's dreaming of me.

In my bed.

With her hand between her thighs.

While murmuring my name.

How the fuck am I supposed to resist this? I demand. *Or am I meant to join?*

It feels like a test.

A *trial.*

This female is meant to be my queen. If she needs attention, I will give it to her. Because she owns every part of me.

My heart. My body. My soul.

"I'm here, pet," I say, kneeling on the bed beside her. "Now spread your thighs so I can see how swollen you are."

Even in her sleep, she obeys, her legs falling open as she presents her slick pussy for my view. She has three of her own fingers inside herself, but her brow is pinched in frustration.

"It's not enough, is it?" I ask, amused. "You want something thicker, don't you, regina mea?"

I have half a mind to free my cock and give her exactly what she needs.

But Marius's words haunt me. I need to make this about *her* pleasure, not mine.

My lips twist. Perhaps the solution is to delay my gratification and wait until she demands that I take my lust out on her.

A jolt of heat settles in my groin at the concept, the notion one I find very pleasing. *Does that defeat the purpose?* I wonder.

I'm supposed to be focused on her, not myself.

Yet everything involving her pleases me.

"Fuck it," I mutter, sprawling out beside my writhing female. "You need me. That's all that matters now."

Because she appears to be in pain, her fingers not doing what she needs. The tip of my tail trails up her athletic leg, and a soft gasp leaves my intended's lips. I wait to see if she'll wake, or react in—

Her hand leaves her pussy and wraps around my appendage, her slick fingers drawing a hiss of exquisite need.

"Gods, pet," I say, feeling instantly pained. "You're *soaked.*"

I can see the glistening flesh. It's like a beacon between her thighs begging me to lick her clean. But I'm frozen in shock as she guides my tail to her entrance instead.

Heat shoots up from my tip, searing my nerve endings. "Fuck," I pant, nearly coming from the stroke of her palm as she pushes me into her sweet cunt.

A beautiful moan leaves her, and suddenly she's rolling into my body.

I cup her cheek, trying to see if she's awake, but she buries herself in my chest and begins to move against me.

She's fucking my tail.

I don't stop her. I simply flare the end and stroke that place I know she likes. When her leg comes up and over mine, I move my hand down to her ass and hold her as she rides me.

"That's it, my queen," I whisper. "Take what you need."

This is the beginning of the famous mating high, I realize.

Gods, I've heard about this. Have craved it for eternity.

But it shouldn't be happening yet. This experience is meant to happen *after* our official mating.

"Fuck, pet," I breathe, feeling her clamp down around me.

If this is the mating heat, then my human pet is going to be insatiable soon. It'll be my duty to see her through the pending heat-like experience. Just as it will be her job to accept my lust.

I bury my face in her hair and inhale her sweet perfume. She nuzzles my chest, her hands clinging to my shirt.

And then she detonates around my tail, her orgasm so intense that I feel it through our growing bond.

It has my cock straining in response, my balls ready to fucking explode.

But then she quiets with a sigh, and her body goes placid against mine. Like all that pent-up need has fled her system and she can finally rest.

However, she holds my tail in place, her grip the only firm thing about her.

If she wants to sleep with me inside her, I won't fight the urge. In fact, I encourage it instead—by widening my tip and lodging it within her slick channel.

She releases another sound of contentment, her body seeming to snuggle even more into mine. Then she falls into a deep slumber.

With my tail in her pussy.

It's beautiful. Right. *Perfect.*

Closing my eyes, I let her hold me in this state, and force myself to ignore my raging need. *This is for her, not me,* I think. *When she's ready, I'll unleash my passion. Until then… we'll sleep.*

CHAPTER FIFTEEN
VIVI

I FEEL FULL.

Replete.

Sexually satisfied.

But there's something between my legs that's making me want more. It's… it's strange. I'm not even sure where I am or when I fell asleep. But I know I've been dreaming of sex.

Of *him*.

God, I always dream of Count Negru. I'm obsessed with a figment. A vampire. A—

"I'm a Strigoi, Viviana," a deep voice murmurs, the rumble of it next to my ear. "Stop thinking of me as a vampire. We're different creatures. And I already told you that the title of *Count* is beneath me, too. It's *King*, pet. Or Ciprian… with you."

I forget how to breathe as reality comes crashing down around me.

Memories of… I'm not sure if they're from yesterday or earlier today… assault my mind.

Sucking Ciprian's cock. Being on my knees for what felt like hours. Talking about mating bonds. Trials. *Breeding*.

My insides clench, and a moan escapes me at how good it feels. There's something inside me. *His tail*, I realize, my hand clenching the root.

I dreamt about this—about putting him inside me and riding his triangle tip.

It was real.

Oh God… I pleasured myself with his appendage… while I slept.

Opening my eyes, I find myself curled into his chest, his soft dress shirt pillowing my face.

My interior muscles pulse again, drawing another sound from my lips. It's needy. It's intense. It's… it's shameless.

He used my mouth. Why can't I use his tail? It only seems fair.

"You can use whatever part of me you desire, my queen," he tells me softly. "That includes my tongue… if you prefer it."

Every part of me spasms in response, my body instantly craving his.

He's bewitched me somehow. Seduced me. *Possessed me*.

But I don't have enough activated brain cells to care.

I pull back and reach for him, needing to kiss him. He's there before I even finish the thought, his tongue spearing into my mouth with a dominant stroke I feel all the way to my toes.

Then his tail begins to move, and my grasp on reality fades. All I can do is feel. Experience. *Survive*.

His palm finds my breast, his thumb teasing my nipple and sending sparks through my system. I'm on fire. Burning away to ash. *Needing him to help me fly*.

"Please," I whisper against his mouth, not sure what I desire, but knowing I need more. "Please, Ciprian."

He kisses a path down my neck as his fingers unfasten the buttons of my shirt. I almost forgot I was wearing it since my lower half is so openly exposed. But now I feel the fabric bunched around my hips. However, it lessens as he pulls the material apart to expose my breasts.

I shiver, then gasp as he seals his mouth around one stiff peak. Two sharp points press against my sensitive skin but don't break the surface. It's a tease. A request. *An insane need.*

All I can do is say "*Yes.*" I want to feel him bite me. Mark me. *Drink from me…*

He takes hold of my nipple and sinks his fangs into my flesh.

I scream, the pinch sending me spiraling into a whirlwind of dark oblivion, one that refuses to end as he *feasts*.

I can't tell if I'm awake or dreaming. It feels too fantastic to be real. But as he releases my breast to move to the other, I catch glimpses of his room, the setting grounding me for a blink before he bites my opposite peak and begins to drink again.

He's marking me. Feeding from me. *Making me his…*

And his tail is moving inside me, forcing me to take more, going deeper, thickening, *preparing me* for his cock. I can sense the intention, and I'm not mad about it.

I should be.

God, our last conversation… I was too exhausted by my mental state to consider everything he was saying. I asked for a moment of space and fell asleep. In his bed. I barely remember it.

How long was I asleep?

Almost fifteen hours, he replies into my thoughts, reminding me that we're mentally linked.

We're bound together by blood, fated to possibly become mates.

If I can pass the trials.

He explained Strigoi culture and expectations to me, telling me how they test potential candidates for the Strigoi King.

I'm the first potential candidate.

The first human he's ever desired.

"What about a Strigoi female? Can she become a Strigoi Queen?" I asked him yesterday.

"Only if she's born royal." He cupped my cheek then as he added, "If our firstborn is female, then she will one day become a Strigoi Queen, and she will take a human as a mate. That mortal would go through trials, too."

I shiver, recalling other things he told me.

Like how Strigoi only take humans as mates. And pairings are not always male-female, either.

"I've tested men," he informed me. "There's something about their scent, though, that never appealed to me. So I primarily focused on women in my hunt for an intended. However, no one intrigued me… until you."

It's romantic in a way. Scary in another.

Because I'm the first and only mortal in over a thousand years that he's wanted more than blood from.

The way he's drinking from me now confirms how starved he is for companionship. His tail is so deep in me that I swear I feel the tip in my stomach.

I don't, but… but it's… it's intense.

"Ciprian," I whisper, trying to ground myself. To focus. To… to… I don't know. Regain a semblance of control? "I…"

He lifts his mouth from my breast, my blood painting his lower lip.

At least until he licks it clean.

His eyes are a glowing crimson, his hair a wild mane of dark colors that hides his pointed ears. But he's not human. That much is very clear. And not just because of the wings at his back or the tail inside me.

Yet all I want is to be held by him. Kissed by him. *Penetrated by him.*

I feel drugged. Pent-up. Needy.

He crawls back up my form, his bat-like wings splaying across the bed as his size becomes incredibly evident. He's so much bigger than me. So much stronger. But all of that just makes me want him more, not less.

"Did you decide on a safe word?" he asks, his question nearly undoing me.

Because this ancient monster is actually trying to understand me. He's *listening* to what I have to say. He may have been rough. He may have hurt me. But on some level, he obviously cares… because he's attempting to do right by me.

And that knowledge has me grabbing him and kissing him.

He lets me, his tongue gliding with mine in a passionate embrace that almost allows me to feel like his equal. *Almost.* However, his massive form and the strength of it have me feeling very petite beneath him.

I like it.

I like him.

I like *this*.

"Vampire," I breathe.

He growls in response. "*Strigoi.*"

"No," I whisper, shaking my head. "*Vampire* is my safe word. If I say it, you stop."

He stares down at me. "What if you think it?"

My lips twist. Because he has a point. I woke up thinking about him being a vampire. "I have to say it out loud."

"And if your beautiful mouth is otherwise occupied?" he asks silkily, one of his eyebrows arching.

I swallow, which draws his attention to my throat. It doesn't take a blood-bond or mind reading to determine what he's thinking. "If I… can't speak, then I'll hold up two fingers in a V shape?" I suggest awkwardly.

His lips twitch. "What if your hands are bound?"

An image flashes through my head, one of me on my knees with my wrists tied behind my back and his cock deep in my throat. "If you incapacitate me, then you need to be focused on my mind and what I'm thinking," I tell him. "If I think *vampire* on repeat while we're in the middle of, um, *things*, that should be enough, right?"

He cups my jaw, his thumb tracing the hollow beneath my eye as he holds my gaze. "Yes, regina mea. I believe that would be a sufficient way to ensnare my attention."

"Okay. Then *vampire* is my safe word."

His tail stops moving between my legs. "Are you using it right now?"

"No."

"Then I may continue?"

My cheeks warm. "Yes, please."

"Hmm," he hums, his focus slipping down to my mouth. "I think you were right before, Ms. Dalca. I rather like hearing you *consent*."

"Then you're going to love it when I beg," I whisper, my hips pushing into his and driving his tail deeper. "Make me come again, King Negru. *Please*."

A rumble ignites in his chest, part growl and part purr. "With my tail or my tongue?"

"Both?" I ask, feeling hot all over.

"Call me Ciprian again, and I'll do whatever you desire, Viviana."

The heat from my cheeks spreads down to my neck. "Can you pleasure me with your tongue and your tail, Ciprian?"

His gaze narrows to a smolder, the crimson flecks overtaking the obsidian color. "Do you promise not to move?"

I nod. "Yes."

"Then I shall… *learn*." The tip of his tail expands inside me, nearly making me jump. But his weight holds me down. "Breaking promises already?"

"Not intentionally," I breathe, fighting the urge to writhe as his appendage moves inside me.

His dark eyebrow wings upward. "Do I need to hold you down, sweet queen of mine?"

My throat works and I nod again. "I think so, yes."

"Hmm," he hums, then begins kissing a path downward. Goose bumps pebble down my arms as he nears my mound, my mind recalling how it felt to be bitten down there.

I'm not sure I'm ready for that again. It was so intense. And he… he didn't *stop*. What if he does it again? What if he accidentally takes too much this time?

Shh, he hushes into my mind. *I'm not going to bite you again until you ask me to.* He presses a kiss to my clit just as his hands grab my hips to hold me down. It's a good thing he caught me, or I would have jolted again.

It seems that staying still is impossible.

Especially with his tail doing… doing whatever it's doing inside me.

And, oh God, his mouth…

His tongue is against my…

"*Ciprian,*" I moan, fisting the covers as my legs strain beneath him. I want to shift my hips. To ride his face. His tail. *Him*. He's only just begun, and I'm nearly out of my mind with lust. Nothing like this has ever happened to me. It's like I'm insatiable.

Didn't I just come a few minutes ago?

God, have I been coming all night?

My insides feel overheated, like I've recently climaxed… a lot more than *once*.

Five times throughout the fifteen hours, he says into my mind. *So not too many times.*

Five times while I was asleep is a lot of times, I say, moaning out loud as he sucks on my sensitive nub. *God, don't stop.*

Then call me Ciprian, not God. Or, if you must use a formality, then "mate" would be nice.

The possession underlying his tone has me shuddering, my heart racing in my chest. *I feel possessed.*

Me too, regina mea. Me too. He punctuates the words by tonguing my clit as he strokes my G-spot with his tail.

I'm a slave to the sensations. A slave to his touch. A slave to his *mouth*.

I don't inch closer to the edge—I soar right off of it, his name leaving me on a scream as I experience what might just be the most intense orgasm of my life.

I black out.

Return to reality.

Only to fall into a spiral of oblivion so overwhelming that I forget how to breathe.

He must notice or be concerned, because in a blink, he's forcing air into my mouth as he continues to drive me deeper into my rapturous cyclone.

It's a delirium of passion, one I feel may kill me. But I don't care. Not when I feel like this. Not when I have his strong body around me, holding me while I fall apart.

I breathe him in.

Exhale.

And inhale his scent again.

Vanilla and lavender.

Monster and man.

I'm drunk on him. Lost to our embrace. Loving every second.

Until finally, the world begins to tilt into view again. The canopy over his bed. The dark silks and mahogany wood. The chandelier in the center of the room.

"Your bedroom is a Gothic wet dream," I tell him on a sigh. "I like it here."

"That's good to hear," he murmurs, his chest to my back as he holds me on the bed. I don't know when I rolled to my side or how he ended up spooning me, but I don't mind. It feels nice. "The Strigoi Kingdom is similar to this."

"It is?"

"Yes." He presses a kiss to my neck. "I've not been back often, but I've seen it evolve. The technology of your realm is behind, and there are parts of this world that are vastly different from my home. However, I think you'll find some similarities to help you adjust."

My brow furrows. We discussed some of the trials and what they meant, but not me agreeing to partake… or go to the Strigoi Realm. "You're speaking as though a decision has been made."

"Because it has," he says, his voice stoic… *stern*. "Marius informed me last night that the trials have already begun. He was the first test. Congratulations, you passed."

CHAPTER SIXTEEN
CIPRIAN

I HOLD MY BREATH, waiting for her reaction to what I've just revealed.

When she remains quiet for too long, I frown. "Viviana?"

"Yes?"

"Are you all right?" I ask, shifting so I can roll her to her back and stare down at her.

She blinks up at me. "I'm processing."

"Oh." I suppose that's better than hearing her say *vampire*. It's also better than her screaming or crying. I know she understands, at least on the surface, how important these trials are for my kind. But I don't think she's aware of the risks.

I'm also aware that she didn't actually consent to them, either. Something I assume will bother her, given her previous comments on the topic.

"If it matters, I did not initiate the trials. At least, not directly." I study her beautiful face as I slowly retract my tail.

She doesn't move, just continues to look up at me as her mind considers everything I've told her over the last few days.

"Marius says my people felt my intentions," I go on. "They're impatient. Which is my fault for taking so long to find a worthy candidate. I would apologize for that, but there's a reason I chose to be selective. I don't want to fail."

"Fail in providing a good, uh, bride…?" she asks.

"A good candidate, yes. And I don't want to fail my mate either," I say, sitting up and moving to lean against the headboard. "Previous rulers have chosen to use the trials as a matchmaking game."

That's the best way I can describe the behavior.

But it's not quite accurate.

"As I mentioned, the humans in my world know Strigoi exist." I informed her of that when discussing the trials and the importance for my world. "So a contest typically ignites among the mortals to… *auction* brides."

Viviana moves on the bed to join me by the headboard, my shirt still clinging to her arms yet hanging open to reveal her perfect form.

I try to ignore the allure, but it's difficult.

However, I need her to understand this—the importance of what she means to me. *Why* it's taken me so long to find her. *How* I ended up in this world.

"Are the auctioned brides usually willing?" she asks, her dark eyes holding mine.

"Yes. Always. Because becoming queen in my world is a coveted position."

"Becoming a queen in this world is also coveted, I think," she replies. "Wealth. Power. It's something a lot of humans desire."

I nod. "I've noticed that throughout the centuries.

However, I've avoided monarchs and their frivolous politics by making payments and using compulsion." I study her. "Though, sometimes a clever mortal stumbles upon records of my existence."

"How do you usually handle those *clever mortals*?" she asks.

"I send them on a path that leads them elsewhere."

She waits for me to elaborate, and I can hear in her mind that she's wondering if anyone else has ever arrived at my doorstep.

"You're the first outsider that I've allowed to learn my secret," I murmur. "Only the staff in my home are aware of who and what I am, and their families have helped safeguard me for many generations."

"So Marius is… a descendant?"

I smirk. "Marius isn't human, Viviana. He's a Strigoi. My second-in-command, actually. And my best friend."

Her eyes widen more and more with each statement I make. "So he's not a familiar?"

"Strigoi don't have *familiars*, pet. We have staff. We have humans who allow us to feed. And, well, some of us have harems, too. Marius, for example, has very much enjoyed being the acting monarch in the Strigoi Kingdom. Which I suppose brings me back to the *auctions*—Marius has received many humans as gifts. All of them wishing he would take one as a mate."

"But he has a harem instead," she says slowly.

"Precisely."

"So you, too, could have a harem?" The wariness in her tone tells me how she feels about this concept. And the wave of possessiveness coming from her thoughts almost makes me smile.

"Yes, I could," I admit. "However, I've never desired a

harem. I've always wanted to find a mate, not dally with inconsequential relations. Which is why I left my home world and came here. I craved someone different. Someone unique. Someone… not offered up on a platter for potential slaughter."

I go on to reiterate the purpose of the trials, how my kind tests potential mates for Strigoi royals.

"They have to approve of their king and queen," I stress. "It's widely understood in my realm and accepted as a challenge among the mortals. My predecessors enjoyed the carnage. At least until one of them fell for a candidate who died."

It's not a story I like to think about, yet it's one that haunted my childhood.

Because that candidate was my mother's older sister.

"The trials are about testing a human's worth as the mother or father of a royal heir. So many of the tasks focus on stamina and strength, the goal being to ensure that whoever procreates with a Strigoi is capable of adding impressive traits to the match."

It makes sense from an evolutionary standpoint. But it's an archaic practice.

I've always felt that I should be trusted to pick an appropriate mate. And that's mostly why I set off on my own to find someone worthy of the task.

Instead, I found boredom. Complacency. *Irritation.*

No one ever felt right.

Until now.

There has to be a reason for that. Viviana is different. I can feel it in my soul. *If the Strigoi reject her…*

It's a thought I don't let myself finish.

And instead focus on sharing all of this out loud, telling her why I ventured here to find my own mate. How my father allowed the Strigoi and humans of our realm to engage in a series of trials for entertainment.

"He didn't want to pick any of the candidates himself, so he allowed it to be turned into a spectacle." My tone is flat to mask my anger.

It was a reckless choice.

Over fifty mortals lost their lives because he didn't care enough to vet them before letting them fight for a chance at the throne.

"My father didn't want to waste time on a decision that wasn't truly his to make, but then he met Shyla. She changed everything for him."

My mother always said it was love at first sight between them.

I assume now that she meant *lust* at first sight.

"He chose Shyla and presented her as his queen. But the Strigoi weren't finished with their tests. Ultimately, she failed."

She more than failed; she *drowned*. Which I explain to Viviana next because she needs to understand the dangers of the trials.

"They tested her stamina by making her tread water for hours," I mutter. "She drowned."

I suspect it was exhaustion-related, as my father probably kept her up all night the evening before. Perhaps even used her that morning.

I don't know for sure, and I'll never ask. But if my need for Viviana is any indication, I can understand his hunger being the culprit for Shyla's failure.

"He was… disappointed after her death. He almost canceled the trials entirely, stating that he wanted to try again after a new generation of humans revealed itself." Meaning he wanted to wait another century or so to begin again. "But Shyla's parents suggested a new candidate. A candidate who became my mother."

I explain that she was Shyla's younger sister by two years and wasn't originally chosen to participate. Then, after everything that happened, she was thrust into the spotlight and left with little choice in the matter.

"She won, I think, because my father revered her and refused to touch her. He felt guilty about what happened to Shyla, which is why I strongly suspect he was the reason for her fatigue in the trials." I shake my head. "Anyway, this history impacted my decisions. I'm not interested in a public spectacle."

That's why I've always intended to present a candidate of my choosing to the Strigoi, only after I properly prepared the human for the trials ahead.

Alas, it appears my careful planning has been thwarted by my people.

"The Strigoi can adapt and change," I tell her. "But some traditions are… resolute. And it seems they've felt my interest in you for a while now. According to Marius, they're done waiting. We have less than a week to prepare."

"And no choice in the matter," Viviana adds, finally speaking after listening to me talk for… a while.

"I would apologize, but we're destined. The moment I learned of your existence, our fate was set. That's the only explanation for my mounting obsession." I lean forward to cup her cheek, needing to feel her. "I've never desired another this way. You are meant to be mine."

I refuse to believe otherwise.

My original assumption that I would just play with her and discard her was founded on my need not to hope.

She changed all that the moment she stepped into the dining room. Her scent. Her confidence. Her intelligence.

Her lack of fear. They were all traits that left me spellbound. And it's a spell I refuse to break free from.

"I've obsessed over you for years," she confesses after a long beat of silence. "Your myth. Your existence." She stares into my eyes. "I knew there would be consequences for finding you. But I never worried about them. I just… I had to find you."

"Had you not come for me, I would have come for you," I tell her. "The only reason I waited was because I wanted to see how far you would go to reach me."

"Marius helped," she says.

My lips twitch, the action feeling oddly familiar now—because of her. Her influence. Her presence. The way she makes me feel. I never smiled before. Now I seem unable to stop. "I thought he was doing me a favor. Turns out, his assistance was never about me—it was about *you*."

"The first trial," she replies.

"Yes." Or maybe it happened the morning I sent him in to test her. I'm not quite sure. And honestly, it doesn't matter. Focusing on the past is a waste of time. We need to move forward. "He has told the Strigoi that I want a week to prepare you. That was yesterday, which means we have six days. Potentially less… if they refuse to wait."

"Will he give us a warning?"

I shake my head. "I'm rather certain that his informing me of the first trial is the only version of a warning we will receive. My Strigoi are impatient to meet their future queen. They've been without one… for a while."

She frowns. "So how does royalty work in your world?" she asks slowly. "I mean, you're immortal and you live forever… right? Same with your mates?"

"Yes, Strigoi are immortal, as are our mates. But that doesn't mean we can't die."

This is the part of my history that I never discuss with anyone. Not even Marius.

But Viviana deserves to know.

So I clear my throat and push forward with the truth.

"Royalty changes typically involve a monarch passing the title on to an heir via a ceremony. However, in my case, I inherited the title much earlier than expected. After my mother killed herself, my father went insane. And I was left in charge of all of Strigoi kind at the age of eighteen."

CHAPTER SEVENTEEN
VIVI

The emotionless way Ciprian recounts his past suggests he has no heavy feelings regarding his history. However, his dedication to forgo standard trial practice tells me how he truly feels.

He spent over a thousand years hunting for the right candidate, choosing to renounce his kind's customs in favor of creating a new tradition.

One that has culminated in him finding me.

"Mates share everything," he explained shortly after mentioning his mother's suicide. "Every thought. Every feeling. Every *regret.*" He stopped looking at me then, choosing to stare across the room as he added, "My mother knew how my father felt about her sister. He loved Shyla. And… my mother looked just like her."

I didn't need him to tell me what came next because I already knew.

Yet he said it anyway. "My father pretended my mother was Shyla. He even called her by that name, forever reminding her that she was never his true choice. Yet they were mated. Because the Strigoi chose her."

He went on to tell me that his father hated the Strigoi for that decision. He blamed Ciprian's mother, too. And that… led to a bleak future.

"Shortly after I turned eighteen, I found my mother hanging from the balcony." He didn't go into much detail after that, just said that the memory is one that would haunt him forever.

It sounded like a warning—a way of letting me know that it would soon haunt me, too. *Once we're mated.*

But I'm not intimidated by his past or his mind.

I am, however, nervous about these *trials*. They're clearly dangerous. And his Strigoi have waited a long time to vet a potential queen. Far longer than normal, from what he just explained to me at the dining table.

We've been talking since I woke up in his bed, only recently relocating downstairs for a meal.

It's very different from my first few days here when he seemed obsessed with putting his tail inside me. Now he's focused on teaching me everything.

Because we're on a deadline.

I should probably be freaked out. Terrified. Demanding that he let me go.

However, I'm none of those things. I'm simply lounging in the chair I was meant to sit in the first night here, eating another grilled cheese sandwich.

All while he watches.

"You really should try it," I encourage him, nodding to the gooey deliciousness on his plate.

He frowns down at it. "I can't believe I let you suggest this."

"Consider it my version of a trial," I tell him. "I've yet to really see you eat. Do Strigoi not require food?"

His gaze runs over me, pausing on the buttons of the clean shirt he put on me before bringing me down here.

He didn't opt to change, despite the rumpled nature of his suit. Feeding me was apparently more important than swapping out wrinkled clothes for a freshly pressed outfit.

"I believe I ate you yesterday, Ms. Dalca. And the day before."

I'm not sure if he's referring to drinking my blood or the actions between my thighs. Maybe even both. And just the thought of it sends warmth up my neck. But I distract myself by saying, "I meant food, Ciprian. Do Strigoi need anything other than blood?"

"No." He picks up his glass of wine and takes a drink. "However, we enjoy indulging in flavor, so many of us eat." His gaze goes to my breasts before slowly traveling up to my face. "*Frequently*."

"Why do I think you're talking about sex and not a meal?"

Crimson bleeds into his dark eyes. "Because I'm thinking about fucking you on the table." He sets his glass down but doesn't release it. "Eat your sandwich, Viviana. You're going to need your strength."

"For you or for the trials?" I ask, purposely sassing him. It's a nice distraction from all the information floating through my head.

"Both." He swirls the contents of his glass, his gaze assessing. "I have no idea what to expect from the trials. It's never been done this way before. Nor has it ever taken this long for a mortal to be tested."

"Yes, you said you've been hunting for… a millennium."

He dips his chin. "Most trials happen within a century of a Strigoi assuming the royal title. But I spent my first hundred years restoring order to a broken kingdom. Between my mother's death and my father's mind breaking along with his heart, there was a lot of panic and uncertainty."

Ciprian takes another sip of his wine, his gaze falling to his plate.

"This is a part of my life that I never speak about, Viviana. I'm only trying to ensure you understand why my people may be hard on you. They're eager for me to take a queen. No one has ever taken this long to accept a mate. No one has ever left our world to hunt for one either." He looks at me again, his gaze seeming to search mine.

"I'm not afraid," I tell him.

"I know. Which makes you unique in this world and perfect for mine. Because the humans in my world are not afraid either." He studies me for a moment. "Actually, we should discuss this more. I've told you how Strigoi protect humans and how humans feed Strigoi. But I haven't mentioned the venom exchange yet."

The bite I just took seems to stick to my mouth as I stare at him. *Venom exchange?* I ask via my mind since speaking would be difficult at the moment.

"Strigoi bites have a venom in them that actually makes humans somewhat immortal in my world. So they're referred to as *immortals* back home. But they're not truly immortal, not the way a Strigoi is. They're just… less breakable. And they live longer."

I start chewing because I need access to my voice to ask some questions.

But he keeps speaking, telling me how his venom hasn't reacted that way in humans here, how every person he's bitten has lived a normal life. "At least, as far as I know," he adds. "Which did make me wonder for a while if I could even mate one of your kind."

He continues by saying that his doubts were answered

the moment I imbibed his blood because everything inside me has reacted the way it should.

Which means we're compatible, just as he always suspected.

"It simply seems my venom works a little differently on the humans of my world than on the ones here. But I thought you should be aware of the venom exchange process, as you're going to hear the term 'immortals' in the Strigoi Kingdom, and I didn't want you to be confused."

I finished chewing a few minutes ago, but he kept talking, answering inquiries before I could even think them through.

"The blood exchange provides true immortality, though," he goes on. "Three exchanges, to be precise. Which is why I can't give you my blood again. Not until after the trials." His eyes meet mine as he adds, "You'll go into a heat. The instinct to breed will be too much. And unlike what Marius suggested the other day, I do not intend to cheat the trials."

Whoa, I think, holding up a hand. "Okay, hold on. *Heat?*" I'll come back to the *cheating* comment in a moment. "I'm going to experience a… a *heat?*"

"Yes." He nudges his untouched plate to the side and leans forward. "And it's going to push me into a rut."

"A rut," I repeat, aware of the term but wondering if I'm understanding it correctly. "Meaning you're going to… *rut* me."

"Absolutely. For days, I hope. But my blood running through your veins will strengthen you enough to survive my hunger. Which is why I wanted you to understand the immortality aspect of our bond. It means you'll heal from whatever I do to you. So just try to enjoy it. I know I will."

"Okay, that…" I trail off as a fire ignites inside me.

This should *not* intrigue me.

And it certainly should not be making me burn all over.

"Ciprian," I whisper, swallowing. "Let me make sure I… understand. We can't mate until I survive the trials. Then our mating is going to send me into a heat. You'll, um, rut me, and I'll end up pregnant with an heir. Right?"

"Yes." His expression practically smolders as he looks at me. "I have a thousand years' worth of pent-up lust for you to handle, pet. Which means we need to work on your stamina."

My nipples tighten in response to his words. "You did say strength and stamina are part of the trials."

"They are."

"So how would you recommend I train?" I voice the question coyly, aware that I'm flirting with a monster. Aware that he looks ready to eat me. Aware that I'm probably insane for choosing any of this.

But I'm just as obsessed with him as he is with me. Perhaps even more so, as I flew all the way here just to hunt him.

It might be fate.

It might be an enchantment of some kind.

Or maybe… maybe this is simply my purpose in life. To become a Strigoi King's pet. His mate. His queen.

He growls, clearly hearing my thoughts. "Take off that shirt," he tells me. "Leave it on the chair. *And run.*"

"Is this a training exercise?" I ask, standing slowly as I begin unbuttoning the shirt. "Something to help me handle the trials?"

"Sure," he answers vaguely. "We'll consider it an introduction to a rut. But unlike later, I'm going to be kind and give you a two-minute head start. Feel free to go outside, if you prefer. Hide, too. See if you can outsmart me, regina mea."

"Technically, I'm not your queen yet," I say, teasing him a little. Though, admittedly, I really do like that endearment. "Right now, I'm just your pet." Which I can't believe I just said after recently explaining to him my feelings on being referred to as such.

However, it feels appropriate for the moment.

And while it's a little demeaning, I do enjoy the dark affection that seems to underscore his tone when he refers to me as his pet.

"So catch me if you can, my king." I drop my shirt on the chair and smile as his heated gaze roams over my naked state. "Maybe I'll even let you fuck me."

He growls as I turn toward the door. "You won't *let* me do anything to you, Ms. Dalca. You're mine. And I'll fucking take whatever I want from you."

It's on the tip of my tongue to remind him of my safe word. But I decide to see how this plays out.

Either he'll respect me.

Or he'll prove himself to be a monster.

Regardless, this is my fate now. My game to play. *My trial.*

"Start counting," I tell him.

And then… *I run.*

CHAPTER EIGHTEEN
CIPRIAN

MY FEMALE IS AROUSED.

I can smell her. Hear her heart racing. *Feel her.*

This isn't a fair chase. Our link allows me to sense her with ease, my nose tracking her delicious scent all the way out the front door and into the nearby woods.

It was a bold choice running out here in the cold. An even bolder choice heading toward a forest renowned for its brown bear population.

Of course, none of those predators lurk near my castle. Their noses warn them from miles away of my presence.

And I'm a much scarier beast than they will ever be.

A beast who is now hunting his desired prey.

Her citrus aroma is tanged with copper, telling me she scraped herself somewhere along the way, drawing blood.

On purpose? I wonder, my chest rumbling in response. *Or did she hurt herself while fleeing?*

I suppose the *why* doesn't matter. I'll be punishing her for wasting her essence regardless of the reason.

Her blood belongs to me. As does her sweet cunt. Her beautiful mouth. And that body meant for my kind of sin.

Gods, I'm so fucking overstimulated that it's almost difficult to walk. I really should have removed my suit, but I rather like keeping her naked while hiding my body from her view. Plus, the challenge of being agile while hard is… exciting.

I move across the ground, my dick throbbing with every step.

I don't run. I walk. *Hunt.* Trailing after my female's alluring fragrance.

She's close.

She's hiding.

She's waiting.

A purr ignites in my chest, my beast pleased that I haven't spotted her yet. It means she's actually trying to play this game. It's one she's destined to lose, but that's not the point. Strigoi love a good hunt.

And I've never had cause to play.

Prowling forward, my wings tuck up against my back, my movements soundless along the earth.

Are you wet for me, pet? I whisper into her mind. *Maybe you should start pleasuring yourself, ensure you're ready to take me. Because I'm not going to be gentle with you.*

Good. I don't want gentle, she replies, her sultry voice warm inside my head.

I adore this link to her. It's not what I expected, but it's what I need to become a better mate for her.

I'm learning. She's learning. And together—

A chill runs down my spine, causing me to freeze mid-stride. "Viviana?" Instinct pulls her name from my mouth, my gaze narrowing through the trees.

Her scent was a beacon mere seconds ago, her heartbeat an enticing rhythm in my ears.

Then both disappeared.

"Viviana?!" I shout, spinning as I search for her

existence in the forest.

But I sense nothing. Hear nothing. Feel *nothing*.

It's like she's dead.

Or gone.

A roar rumbles through me, my wings spreading in an ominous wave of energy as my hands curl into fists. "*Where is she?*" I demand, rotating toward an approaching presence. "You gave us seven days, Marius. *Seven*. It hasn't even been one."

"I told you I would take the request back to the Strigoi. They rejected it."

"They *rejected* it?" The echoed words leave me on a growl. "*I* am their *king*. They cannot *reject* my demand."

"The trials are not yours to dictate," he replies, his voice calm. "It's time to come home, Ciprian."

My jaw cracks from being clenched so hard.

I should have anticipated this. Should have realized that my Strigoi would never give me more time with Viviana.

They want to ensure she's the right candidate before I take this too far and finalize our connection.

Because a dead mate can incapacitate a king. They witnessed that with my father, his insanity renowned through the Strigoi Kingdom.

He lost the other half of his soul, and he never recovered.

They housed him in an isolated estate where he'll wallow for eternity, regretting his choices. Regretting his past. Wishing for an alternative. All while living within the cage of his mind.

I was trying to avoid such a future for myself, my desire to pick a worthy human paramount to all else.

But the Strigoi clearly don't trust my instincts. They have to test the results for themselves.

"*She's my queen,*" I snarl at Marius.

"I agree," he says. "However, the Strigoi need to be sure. Besides, we both know it's better this way. You're growing attached, and while your control is better than that of anyone else I know, even you have limits, Cip."

His use of that damn nickname nearly has my fist meeting his face. "Now isn't the time, *Mars*."

"True. Your mate has entered her second trial." He cants his head, sending his long hair to the side. "You realize it's not against the rules to also help… yes?"

I stare at him. *Help* isn't something royals typically offer to candidates.

But there isn't anything *typical* about this situation.

"Where's the portal?" I demand, aware that there must be one nearby that ensnared my intended mate. "Take me to her. *Now*."

"Make sure you save some of that sunny disposition for your people," he murmurs, pulling out a device from his pocket.

A device I now realize is a portable portal.

One he must have used to take my mate.

Which means *he* is responsible for her disappearance.

I lunge for him, furious. But he anticipates the move, his hand clasping around my arm with an electric zing. I growl at him. "What—"

"Welcome home." He shoves me forward, causing me to stumble into open air.

My wings stretch on instinct, forcing me to fly before I can truly tumble, and a world of blues, silvers, blacks, and grays reveals itself before me.

The bastard portaled me.

Which was precisely what I needed to do, but the shove was unnecessary.

"Asshole," I mutter, hoping he's behind me.

He doesn't respond. And I don't look at him. I'm too busy searching the palace grounds below.

I haven't visited this place in several years, not since discovering Viviana's existence. She consumed my focus. Became my obsession.

And now she's my *addiction.*

I can feel her again, her mind open to mine as she wanders through a dark forest. She knows she's left the human world, her instincts flaring as she runs for real now.

Before, she was playing.

Now, she's terrified.

I'm here, I whisper to her.

Ciprian, she breathes, her footsteps faltering. I can't hear her movements. However, I can sense them.

Don't stop, I warn her. *I don't know what trial you've entered, but if you're being truly hunted, then you can't stop running.*

This is likely a test of her strength and stamina, just like the one Shyla once failed.

Or perhaps it's about cleverness.

I… I don't know. I have no control. No answers. But I'm here. I can figure out what's happening and try to help her, just like Marius suggested.

I soar through the air, the blood moons above illuminating the ground below. It's always night here, the forestry made of unique fir-like trees that thrive in this realm.

Viviana noticed the difference in horticulture. That's how she realized she'd entered a different world. I can hear the knowledge in her mind, the panic that melted into resolve as she pushed forward.

She didn't freeze out of fear.

She kept going.

Until she heard me.

But now she's sprinting again, convinced someone is chasing her.

My wings beat as I try to find her, to see who and what might be pursuing her.

But the trees surrounding my palace are too dense. I'm not even sure she's in this part of the kingdom.

Fuck.

I fly down to the courtyard out front, where several Strigoi have gathered.

"My king," they greet in unison, bowing.

"Where's my intended?" I demand, not in the mood for formalities or salutations. They took Viviana, and I want her located.

Fjord, the general in charge of my palace security, creates a holographic screen in the air with a wave of one large hand. It pulls up footage of my female—my very *naked* female—running through the woods.

I suppress a snarl, furious that these three men are seeing my woman in this vulnerable state. The anger is made worse by the knowledge that this feed is likely being televised throughout the kingdom.

Which means *everyone* is currently watching Viviana sprint in the nude.

It's not uncommon for the trials. I know this. But that doesn't mean I *like* it.

"Where…?" I trail off, my brow furrowing as I study the background behind my intended. There are fir trees, just like I expected, but the shadowing is all wrong.

I glance up at the moons, note their high positions in the sky, and then look at the screen again.

"That's nowhere near here," I say, confused by the glow coming in at a low angle. It suggests the moons are either just rising or setting.

The endless midnight cycle in this world is unique. But

no amount of time away from it would keep me from recognizing the patterns.

"Marius?" I don't yell my friend's name, just utter it loud enough for him to hear, as I assume he's nearby. He's the one who portaled me here using that handheld device. He must be close. And I suspect I'm going to need that little prized token of his.

"He's still in the other world," Fjord tells me, his silver hair glinting from the moonstream overhead. "He mentioned needing to tie up loose ends."

"Yes, your candidate's home realm doesn't know about supernaturals. Thus, all ties to her existence must be erased. Marius offered to handle the issue." Barnes, a well-respected advisor among the Strigoi, arches an auburn brow at me, daring me to question his wisdom.

He's ancient.

Over five thousand years old.

And he's best friends with my grandfather. Who flanks him on the left, his dark eyes—the same shade as my own—issuing a similar challenge.

But I don't give a fuck about *loose ends.* I wanted Marius's portal device.

He was the one who told me I could *help* my intended, essentially pointing out that there isn't a rule against it. I'm not sure if he meant the suggestion or if he was trying to distract me into traveling here as soon as possible.

Knowing Marius, his comment was layered with both intentions.

Fuck.

I rub a hand over my face as I listen to Viviana consider the path ahead of her. When she starts thinking about a light she's running toward, I frown and look at the holographic screen again.

There's a building in the distance, one that I can barely

make out from the camera they have on my mate. A camera she doesn't appear to be aware of. Our technology is more advanced here. The source of the feed is likely some sort of invisible bug flying alongside her.

Whatever it is doesn't matter.

The structure, however, is important.

Because I recognize it.

It's not a building but a cabin. One I haven't visited in over a thousand years.

My lips part. "No." I look at my grandfather, ignoring the others. "*No.*"

He simply stares back at me. "This is her third trial. If she passes, she will have a break afterward. You're welcome to tend to her then."

"Third trial?" I ask, confused. "What was her second?"

"Your arrival," he states calmly. "Now, I suggest we retreat to the sitting room in the palace. This trial won't be as easy."

He utters the words without emotion. Without care. Without even an ounce of consideration of the danger they just thrust my intended into.

"Viviana Dalca isn't just a candidate. She's my chosen mate," I say, every word clear and concise. "I respect that the Strigoi need to ensure her worth, but this…" I point at the screen. "*This* is suicide."

"Or perhaps it's exactly what we all need," my grandfather replies. "Regardless, I suggest you come with us. If she passes, we'll teleport her here. If she fails, you'll be welcome to retrieve the remains."

My beast roars inside, my fingers curling into fists. "You talk as though she's a pawn in a game."

"Because she is, Ciprian," he answers quietly, stepping into my space. "She's a pawn that may become our queen. But you need to play by the rules and let her lead."

"You've given her no time to prepare. No time to understand. No time—"

"We've waited a millennium for her," he interjects. "And you've had over three years to ready her for these trials. If that wasn't long enough, then neither of you is worthy of your roles in this world."

"Neither of us?" I repeat.

"Be the king you're meant to be," he says, acting as though I didn't speak. "Join us and observe your chosen queen. Or take the next two days trying to fly to her. Your choice."

My teeth grind together.

I can only teleport so far. Typically a few miles at a time. Not *thousands*. It'll only be slightly faster than flying.

And hand portals are rare. That's why I called for Marius. There's only one in the palace, and I assume that's the one he took.

But I'll definitely be checking.

Because if I can reach Viviana, I will.

He told me to help her. *Fucking liar*, I think. He knew I wouldn't be able to stop this or assist her in any way. Not when she's in an isolated part of this world.

An island of trees with a single cabin on the opposite side of the realm.

Fuck.

It's a place of exile.

A home for an insane Strigoi.

My father.

I try to warn her, to tell her who's waiting in that cabin. But we're disconnected again.

And I know why.

There's a force field around that cabin. A force field that keeps my father locked inside.

She's already stepped over the threshold. Which means she's just as trapped as he is.

And so am I, I realize, narrowing my gaze at my grandfather. *Only, I'm trapped* here. *At the palace.*

"Flying to her isn't really an option, is it?" I voice it as a question. But I already know the answer.

He gives me a knowing look. "You're a wise king, Ciprian. Wiser than your predecessors." He starts toward the palace, not bothering to look back at me.

Because why would he?

He's ancient. Just like Barnes.

I understand now that there's a reason Fjord, Barnes, and my grandfather were my welcoming party. One is the general in charge of security, marking him as quite deadly. And the other two are among the strongest of Strigoi kind.

I could fight them, and I might even win.

But I would lose the respect of my kingdom.

And it wouldn't save my intended from the inevitable. It would just make it all worse. It might even guarantee her failure.

Fuck.

There's only one option—let this trial play out.

I chose Viviana Dalca for a reason. Now it's time to see if my instincts about her are right.

But watching her without being able to help her is going to be torture.

Pure. Fucking. Torture.

CHAPTER NINETEEN

VIVI

ISLE OF ISOLATION, STRIGOI KINGDOM

Ciprian? I whisper, feeling a strange sort of aloneness. It reminds me of how I felt when I entered this realm, how I realized quickly that I was no longer in the forest outside of Negru Castle, but somewhere else entirely.

I… I couldn't feel Ciprian.

And I can't seem to sense him now, either.

I didn't even grasp how connected we were until I experienced the severance in our link. Which is how I know something is very wrong now.

But I don't think I've traversed to another realm again.

I'm rather certain I'm still in the Strigoi Kingdom. Although, the log cabin in front of me reminds me of something I might have found in the Hocking Hills back home.

There are a lot of windows overlooking the woods, as well as what appear to be two floors.

And the door is wide open.

My lips twist. *Why does this feel like the beginning of a horror movie?*

Gaby would probably tell me to run and hide. Wait for

Ciprian to come swooping in with his wings and rescue me. Become the damsel in a fairy tale.

Except, no.

That's… that's not the kind of book she would read.

She likes her heroines kick-ass and strong.

I arch a brow. *How ironic.*

I don't feel all that *kick-ass* or *strong* right now. But it's pretty clear that running and hiding isn't an option.

And as for waiting for Ciprian, well…

I close my eyes.

This is obviously a trial. Or I'm in the midst of one, anyway.

So much for having a week to prepare.

Acceptance was never a topic for negotiation. Ciprian chose me. And I'm pretty sure I chose him, too.

The obsession is mutual. The why of it doesn't matter. I'm here. He's somehow cut off from me. So I need to do this on my own.

Pass the trial.

Win the Strigoi King.

Yeah. Okay. Just a walk in the park.

Or, I guess, a walk into the log cabin.

I close my eyes and blow out a breath. "Sure. Yep. Creepy cabin. Entering now." What other choice do I have? Do I run back out into the woods? Pretty certain that would be an instant failure.

They might throw me into an ocean, force me to tread water for eternity or something. That would absolutely suck after the run I've just completed.

I shake my head and open my eyes once more.

Then I step into the cabin.

Nothing happens.

It's silent.

Eerie.

Cold.

Brow furrowing, I move deeper inside. There's a small den to the right, the bookshelves drawing me forward as I read over the unfamiliar titles. "Definitely a different world," I muse, studying the alphabetized novels. "Hmm."

There are no electronics in here. Just a notepad. Some pens. An unlit candle. And a letter knife.

I consider grabbing the last item but decide that would just be foolish. I'm not even sure if Strigoi can die.

Well, that's not true. Ciprian said that his kind are capable of dying. However, he didn't tell me how to kill one.

So.

I'll just… keep wandering.

I find a small living area next, the stairs that head up to the second floor, and a tiny kitchen with a dining nook.

Peering out the back door, I wonder if maybe I've missed the owner. Or if—

"Fresh blood?" a deep voice asks from behind me, the sound of wings fluttering causing my heart to skip a beat.

I turn slowly to find a tall man—a *Strigoi*—with broad shoulders. A perfectly chiseled jaw. Too handsome a face.

Just like Ciprian.

He even has a red tail.

Though, his dark hair is longer. Unkempt. And his irises are pure crimson. Crazed.

I stare at him. Then frown. He's the spitting image of my Strigoi King.

Which can only mean one thing.

"You must be Ciprian's father."

The man—who was prowling toward me—pauses and cants his head. "Ciprian?"

"Your son," I say, holding his gaze. "My intended mate."

He blinks a few times. "Intended mate?"

"Yes."

"You're… a candidate?"

"Yes," I repeat. "The only one." I utter that part with a hint of possession that I don't bother to hide. Ciprian doesn't need any other candidates. He has me. And I—

My back hits the wall harshly, causing the air to leave my lungs as I suddenly find myself pinned by Ciprian's father. His nose is against my throat, his chest rumbling with a growl that renders me temporarily speechless.

It's so different from the rumbles I'm used to from Ciprian. Those make me feel weak. Aroused. *Willing to supplicate.*

But this growl just makes me want to *fight.*

Because it's all wrong.

"Do not bite me," I demand, my voice oddly calm given my predicament. "Ciprian wouldn't like it."

The male doesn't move, just inhales noisily against my neck before pulling back to stare down at me. "You smell like my Shyla."

"No, I smell like your son. Because I'm his chosen mate." I narrow my gaze up at the towering beast. "And his mother's name was not Shyla." That might not be the right thing to say. But I'm going with my instincts here. "You mated her sister." Whose name I don't know. However, I don't voice that out loud.

Not that he would even be able to hear me, anyway, since he's now snarling at me. "You dare speak to me this way, *human*?"

"You're the one who shoved me up against a wall," I point out. "I was being polite until you did that."

He blinks at me. "What?"

"You hurt me." I place my palm on his chest to give him a little shove back.

To my surprise, he moves.

"I don't appreciate being pushed around," I add. "Human or not, I deserve respect. Just like a Strigoi, just like you."

His brow furrows. "Who are you?" he asks, searching my face.

"Viviana Dalca," I say, holding out my hand. "Your son's intended mate."

He glances down at my palm, then back up at my face. "I don't know you."

"No, you don't. That's why I've introduced myself. You are… King Negru?" I voice the name as a guess, assuming he and Ciprian share a last name since they're father and son.

The way the Strigoi straightens his shoulders suggests I was right because a glimmer of pride enters his features, making him even more handsome. "Yes, I am."

"It's nice to meet you." I lower my hand since he doesn't seem all that interested in a handshake. "I believe you're my trial."

"Trial?" His brow comes down. "You dare speak to me about the *trials*?"

The air leaves my lungs once more as I find myself back up against the wall. "*Stop that*," I hiss at him, my body screaming in agony at being shoved not once but *twice*. "I'm in a trial!" I shout at him. "*You* are my trial. Or I assume you are. Did no one tell you?"

He glowers at me. "This is a fucked-up offering. I prefer my blood in bags."

"I'm not an offering," I say through my teeth as he starts scenting my neck for the second time. "I'm your son's intended mate. That's why I smell like him."

King Negru—or former King Negru, or whatever his name actually is—pauses. "Ciprian?"

"Yes."

He slowly pulls away from my throat, his dark wings flaring. "Why are you here?"

I've already answered that, so I try a different route. "The Strigoi wanted me to meet you." Or I assume they did, anyway, since this seems to be a trial of sorts. "I think they want your approval."

It's a solid guess, given how most marriage unions work. Maybe matings operate in similar ways among the Strigoi?

He scoffs. "Why would they care about my approval? They've left me here to *rot*." He shoves away from me and goes to a giant metal box that looks somewhat like a refrigerator.

Only, when he opens it, it's empty.

He reaches inside anyway, making me frown until he pulls out a glass of what looks like blood.

A glass that definitely did not exist a few seconds ago.

"How…?" I trail off and move to join him. "How did you do that?"

"Do what?" He moves to close the door, but I stop him.

"That blood—or I assume it's blood, anyway—appeared out of thin air." I wave my hand inside the fridge, seeing if it's just an illusion. But all I sense is space.

He looks at me, his brow pinched. "What are you doing?"

"Trying to figure out how this thing works," I admit, frowning back at him. "Was the glass disguised or something?"

His long lashes wink at me as his eyes open and close in a slow blink. "You're a confusing human."

"You're a confusing Strigoi," I return. "Well, that might not be fair to say. You're only the third one I've ever met." I return my focus to the still-open fridge and feel the sides of it, continuing my investigative quest. I *will* figure out how this works.

"You have to tell it what to give you," he says slowly. "And what do you mean, I'm the third one you've met? Did you grow up in isolation?" I glance at him to see his expression morphing into surprise. "Is that why you're here? Have the Strigoi finally gifted me with a companion?"

"I… Maybe?" I frown at him. "And when you say I have to tell it what to give me, are you talking about the fridge?"

We stare at each other for a long beat.

"This is… interesting." That's all he says for a moment before adding, "I'm not sure if I like this development or not. You're rather naïve for a human."

"I'm not naïve," I reply, somewhat offended. "I'm just new to this world."

"New how?" he asks, leaning against the counter as he sips his drink.

"Your son found me in a different realm," I explain. "And in my realm, a refrigerator doesn't magically produce glasses of blood."

"It's actually a blutini," he informs me flatly. "Some blood, but mixed with bubbies."

"I…" My brow crinkles. "What are *bubbies*?"

We engage in another staring contest, then he reaches into the fridge and pulls out a bowl of what look like ruby-red berries. "It's a fruit."

"Are they safe for human consumption?" I ask.

"I don't see why they wouldn't be," he replies.

"In my world, some berries are poisonous."

"Oh." He cants his head. "Tell me more about your world."

Before I answer him, I try putting my hand in the fridge again and whisper, "Bowl of human-safe berries, please."

To my shock, one appears right in my hand.

"You don't have to say it out loud," the former king tells me, sounding somewhat amused. "You just think of it and it exists."

"Anything?" I inquire.

Hmm.

"Grilled cheese sandwich like Radu made," I suggest.

When that materializes next, I gasp.

"Holy wow, this is amazing." The words are a whisper to myself, but the Strigoi beside me clearly hears it. Because he makes a choking sound.

Glancing at him, I realize he's chuckling. Or trying to, anyway.

"This does not exist in my world," I inform him. "At least, not that I know of." I frown. "I'm going to be most disappointed if I find out Ciprian has one of these in his castle and didn't show me."

I carry my treasures over to the little dining nook and set them on the table, then return for a magical glass of water, and go to sit.

All while King Negru watches me with an openly curious expression.

"So, you want to hear about my world?" I ask, popping a strawberry into my mouth.

He returns his bowl to the fridge—which causes it to vanish—and joins me. "Yes."

I nod. "All right..."

CHAPTER TWENTY

CIPRIAN

STRIGOI KINGDOM PALACE

I GAPE AT THE SCREEN, dumbfounded.

Viviana is fearless, just talking to my father about her realm, telling him about her studies and how she discovered my existence, and explaining every detail of her life, all without a care in the world.

She even tells him that she prefers to be called "Vivi," something she's never said to me.

I learned about the nickname when researching everything I could find about her existence, but she's not mentioned her preference to me. She only focused on her dislike for *pet*, which I've now learned isn't a true dislike.

Because she definitely responds favorably when I call her *pet* in the right setting.

However, all of this is… mind-boggling. And not just because my intended mate is calmly talking with a psychotic Strigoi, but because that psychotic Strigoi isn't acting all that psychotic.

The last time I saw my father—over a thousand years ago—he could barely string together a sentence, let alone carry on a conversation.

His mind was as broken as his heart and soul, his desire to feed and kill the only two instincts that kept him alive.

When he shoved Viviana up against the wall, everything inside me rioted, my need to escape the palace and get to my mate stealing my breath and nearly causing me to slaughter everyone in the sitting room.

But then he backed off. Because she told him to.

And I… I've been captivated ever since.

This has been going on for hours, the two of them having long since finished their meals. My father is on his fourth blutini glass, and she's gone through several waters.

It's like they're old friends reminiscing. My father even found her a blanket to curl up in when she expressed being cold.

I was relieved when she covered her bare skin, yet furious that she was on display for the entire kingdom for at least an hour before that.

Everyone knows what my mate looks like, which is typical for these proceedings. But it's unacceptable to me. She's *mine*. No one else should be allowed to see her in that manner. Only me.

Though, I can't deny that she resembled a beautiful queen as she conversed and moved with confidence and grace. I warned her that trials are typically broadcast to the kingdom. I'm not sure if she remembered that or not, but at least I did my part in sharing that detail with her.

It's unclear whether or not that makes any of this consensual. Fortunately, she doesn't seem disturbed by the experience. She's merely talking to my father like he's an old friend.

"The general consensus is favorable," Barnes announces, drawing my attention to where he and my grandfather are seated. They've been scanning feedback on their tablets while I watched my intended mate on the holographic screen hovering in the center of the room.

Fjord left us hours ago, choosing to do security rounds instead.

But I know he's here as a babysitter—*for me.*

Which explains the full guard outside.

They were prepared to stop me should I have chosen to intervene. I didn't. However, it wasn't because they intimidated me. I was too captivated by my intended mate to do anything other than observe.

My courageous, beautiful female.

She is positively *stunning.*

All I want to do right now is demand a portal key so I can go to her and pull her into my arms.

Alas, she's still talking to my abnormally sane father.

Or perhaps it's not abnormal at all. Perhaps he's been sane for a while now.

Is that the true purpose of this trial? My grandfather mentioned that this might be the experience we all need.

"Did you know he was of sound mind?" I ask, interrupting whatever Barnes was just saying to my grandfather.

"I've suspected it for some time, yes," my grandfather replies, obviously understanding what I meant by my question. "I don't think he was ever truly insane, just… devastated. We all know Strigoi mate for eternity."

"Yes, but some have taken more than one mate in the past," I say, aware that every dynamic is different. While most of our kind is too possessive to ever share, there are those who prefer it.

"True," he murmurs. "Maybe your father will be one of them in the future. If he's welcomed back into society, I mean."

My eyebrow wings upward. "So this trial was your idea."

He merely smiles. "When you become a father—which I imagine will be soon—you'll understand my decisions, Ciprian."

"Soon?" I echo, caring more about that than his comment regarding my future understanding. I don't need a child to know why he did this.

He wanted to exonerate his son while also proving that my female is the right queen for this kingdom. It's a healing experience. One that will hopefully encourage the Strigoi to trust their royals again.

They need a strong queen, someone who won't break their hearts.

And they needed to rekindle their faith in their former king.

I comprehend all of that now. It was a good idea. If it worked, it was an even better plan.

But I don't care about any of that right now.

I simply want my female. "She's mine to claim," I say before he can respond to my inquiry. Because I don't need him or any of them to tell me that she's passed. I know she's destined to be my queen. "I would like a portal key. Now."

My grandfather's lips twist upward. "I'm surprised it took you this long to demand it."

"Some might consider that a failure," Barnes murmurs conversationally. "However, I'm going to choose to interpret it as a show of respect. He was waiting for a formal decision to be declared before issuing a command."

My grandfather nods. "That's how I choose to interpret it as well."

"Stop talking about me like I'm not fucking here," I growl, pushing to my feet. "She passed. Let me go to her."

The two ancients smile at each other, then stand. "She passed hours ago, based on the feedback we've received. The kingdom is quite taken with your intended mate, Ciprian. But what we haven't told you is that the trials have… evolved."

I stare at my grandfather, waiting for him to elaborate.

However, it's Barnes who says, "After your mother's untimely demise, the elders gathered to discuss future trials. We decided it wasn't fair or enough to merely judge a human's candidacy. Compatibility is the key to success. That's the error we made with your father. And we refused to allow history to repeat itself."

"But then you took it upon yourself to go hunting alone," my grandfather adds. "At first, we were concerned. I almost came after you."

Barnes nods. "Marius intervened."

"He more than intervened. He saved the process," my grandfather replies. "He offered to report back to me with exclusive updates. It was dire there for a while, but he insisted on letting you do this your way. And I'm thankful that we listened."

"Because he was right," Barnes says.

"He was right," my grandfather echoes. "More than right. *This* is how the trials should be conducted—by the Strigoi heir finding his or her own mate, then going through a series of tests to prove their devotion to the other."

"Great. Can I go to her now?" I ask, impatient to leave.

"You're not hearing us," Barnes says.

"I hear you just fine," I argue. "I'm impatient to get to my intended." I hold out a hand. "Now." I don't add a placative word or a plea. It's a demand. These two elders might have incredible power, but I'm the Strigoi King. And I want my female.

"Just continues to prove us right," Barnes murmurs, his amusement grating on my nerves.

"*You* were the primary trial," my grandfather informs me before turning to walk away. "That's what we're trying to tell you, Ciprian."

I stare at his back, irritated by both his words and his physical dismissal. "Are you trying to tell me I failed?"

"Oh, no, you passed," Barnes informs me. "First, with Marius's reports. Second, by storming in here and demanding that we reveal where your mate was located. Third, by respecting your elders while patiently awaiting a verdict."

"And now," my grandfather says, turning toward me once more with a device in his hand, "by commanding that we let you go to your future queen. It proves you're truly enamored with her. Which means you'll do right by her."

"Thus, hopefully, preventing the mistakes of your predecessor," Barnes adds, quieter now.

"Are you telling me all of this has been televised?" I ask, irritated that I've probably been on display for the kingdom this whole time.

But both men shake their heads.

"This was a change devised by the elders, one they required us to report back on—just like Marius did with me. Your reactions were private. Only our feedback will be heard." My grandfather holds out the item in his hand. "Congratulations, Ciprian. I look forward to meeting our new queen."

Barnes steps between us before I can react, making me sigh with annoyance.

I'm very *done* with this conversation and these trials.

All I want is to reach Viviana.

And maybe… maybe pause for a greeting with my father.

"The inauguration will occur in ten days," Barnes informs me, all business again. "That should provide you with enough time to… indulge." With that, he moves again and allows my grandfather to hand me the portal device.

I stare at them both for a beat. "Thank you." I mean it. Mostly because this madness is done. My queen has been approved.

And now…

Now it's finally time for me to claim Viviana as *mine*.

CHAPTER TWENTY-ONE

VIVI

ISLE OF ISOLATION, STRIGOI KINGDOM

"Sorry, I'm not used to, uh, *guests*," the former king says as he hands me a towel from the bathroom doorway. "I'll also try to find you a shirt or something to wear for after your shower."

"That won't be needed," a deep voice says, the sound of it sending a familiar wave of warmth down my spine. "Hello, Father."

King Negru's eyes widen a little as he turns. "Ciprian. I… I didn't hear you…"

"Grandfather gave me a portal key," he says as I try to look around the mass of wings in the doorway. "It's quite useful. Want to borrow it for a bit?"

The bat-like wings in front of me seem to tense. "You would allow me to leave?"

"Under one condition, yes," Ciprian replies. "You attend the inauguration in ten days."

Silence falls between them, and I twist my lips to the side as I set the towel down on the counter.

Should I… leave? I wonder, tightening the blanket around me.

No, regina mea. You're exactly where I need you to be, Ciprian responds into my mind, his mental presence nearly making me sigh with relief.

I missed you, I admit. *Which is crazy. You've been in my head for, like, a day.*

Years, he corrects. *You've been researching me for* years.

True. I smile a little. *I guess you have been in my head for a while…*

"I would be honored," King Negru says, his wings relaxing. "Thank you for inviting me… son."

Another tense moment passes.

"Viviana?" Ciprian murmurs.

King Negru moves, allowing me to finally see my Strigoi. I don't hesitate, just run for him and jump into his arms. He catches me with a growl, then tugs the blanket back around me before it can fall. "Not yet, mate," he tells me. "Father?"

I don't understand what's happening until I'm surrounded by wings, and then we're moving through space in a way my mind struggles to translate. *A portal*, I realize. *We're… we're in a portal.*

Almost there, Viviana, Ciprian replies, his arm strong around my lower back.

I close my eyes and just let him take me.

All of this has been a whirlwind of fate. An experience unlike any I could ever have anticipated. But I would be lying to myself if I didn't acknowledge that I've dreamt of this. Of him. Of the potential that could exist between us.

I thought those fantasies were born of long research hours obsessing over a figment.

But now I wonder if my soul simply knew where I would end up.

Here, in the arms of a Strigoi King, I think, sighing into his embrace.

"We'll see you in ten days," Ciprian announces.

When more than one male chuckle responds to his comment, I peek over his shoulder and see King Negru joining two other men. One of whom looks a lot like Ciprian, too.

My grandfather, Ciprian says into my mind. *The other male is Barnes. Two ancients. They… organized the trials.*

Hmm, I hum. *And I assume you carrying me off like this means… I passed?*

"*We* passed," he says out loud. "Apparently, the rules have changed."

He proceeds to explain everything via a few thoughts, telling me what Barnes and his grandfather shared about testing the royal bloodline along with the human candidate.

It seems like they approved of Ciprian finding his own mate, too.

I'm only vaguely aware of him sweeping me up a staircase, not with his feet but with his *wings*.

We're flying.

However, all I can see is him. His black eyes bleeding with crimson. His square jaw. His thick, dark hair. His… *tail*.

Only, I don't *see* that part of him.

I *feel* it.

"We didn't get to finish our game outside," he says, his lips brushing mine. "I would suggest we play again, but I'm not letting you go, Viviana. You're not just in my nest now. You're in my *kingdom*. And you're never returning to your home world."

My heart races in my chest, my mind whirring with comments.

I wasn't given a chance to say goodbye. To finish my thesis. To… to do much of anything at all.

Yet I don't feel any regret. Nor is there even a hint of sorrow in my thoughts.

I'll miss Gaby. I… I may need to see if I can somehow get her a message. She'll understand this choice. Understand that I fell for a monster eons ago. She knows more than anyone else about my studies. Teased me relentlessly for my research but often commented on how fantastic it would be if I actually found him.

And I did.

I found my Strigoi.

My fixation.

My obsession.

Electricity hums across my skin as Ciprian's tail slides up my inner thigh. He doesn't ask. He doesn't wait. He merely… slips into my waiting heat and claims me from within.

"Already wet for me, hmm?" he hums. "And I haven't heard your safe word, so I assume I have your consent."

He flares that wicked tip, drawing a gasp from my throat.

"I'll take that as confirmation of your approval," he murmurs, then pushes me against a cold wall as water ignites all around us.

A shower, I recognize dizzily.

And instantly I think of our last shower.

How he kept me on my knees.

How he choked me with his cock.

How he just kept *coming*.

Warmth floods my veins, followed by a chill. I'm conflicted. I want this. I want *him*. But I… I don't know if I want *that* right now.

His lips taste mine, his hands peeling away the blanket that's now sticking to me. When he tosses it behind him, I arch a brow. "Are you ever going to let me see you without clothes?"

Even now, he's dressed in an all-black suit, complete with shoes.

Which is ridiculous, given the water raining down on us.

"Do you want to undress me, pet?"

I don't hesitate. "Yes."

"Hmm. And what will you give me as an enticement?"

"Anything you want." It's a bold claim. But this male makes me want to take risks. To forget reality. To simply… *exist*.

His tail drives so deep into me that I see stars. Just for a moment. Then he twirls the tip, and my insides clench.

"I want you aware when I fuck you for the first few times," he says. "Then I'll heal you with my blood, thus finalizing our claim. And I'll rut you until we're both satisfied."

My legs go weak. "I… Will I survive?"

His lips curl into a wicked grin, one that ignites butterflies in my stomach. "With my blood inside you, yes."

"That sounds ominous."

"Because I'm not human, Viviana. You know this." He punctuates his point with… with his *point*. "I intend to claim you in every way imaginable. Pussy. Ass. Your mouth again. I'll fuck you from behind while my tail takes the front. Make you choke on my cock while riding my tip."

His arm is all that keeps me standing as he demonstrates with another twirling motion inside me.

"I'm going to destroy you, regina mea." His lips go to my ear. "And then I'm going to heal you. Again… and again… and again."

He sinks his fangs into my neck, drawing a scream from my mouth.

I can feel his intentions electrifying the air between us, his need a dark beacon that has me quivering against him as I slide down his body. My feet touch the ground, only then reminding me that he's been holding me this whole time. Carrying me like I weigh nothing. Embracing me like I mean *everything*.

"Do you want me to kneel?" I ask.

"No." He palms my cheek, his lips still against my neck as he gently kisses the mark he's left there from his fangs. "I want you to undo my pants, pet. Slowly. *Carefully*." That part is issued as a growl against my throat, one I take to heart as I grab hold of his athletically lean hips.

I've had him in my mouth, his thick length a pulse against my tongue.

Yet something about this makes me nervous. Intimidated. *Excited*.

Because he's giving me permission to… touch him. At least, in my own way. Not as a demand, necessarily. More of an invitation.

And it's one I eagerly accept as I unfasten his belt, pop open the button, and pull down the zipper.

Warmth floods through me as I grasp him with my hand, his cock hot and heavy against my palm. It's not what he told me to do. But his growl of approval goes right to my clit.

"Kiss me," I say, begging him with my words. "Please kiss me, Ciprian."

He draws his lips up to my mouth and claims me in a heartbeat, his tongue mastering mine in a single sweep as he grasps my nape. I moan against him, already lost to the sensations he's unleashing between my legs.

When he grabs one of my breasts, I nearly come apart at the seams.

He has me so pent up, so ready, and this shower just started.

Taking hold of his pants, I push them down, then sigh with contentment as he kicks them off along with his shoes.

But he's still partly dressed.

I don't ask for permission, simply release his dick and start working on his jacket.

It falls to the floor with a wet plop.

Then I go for the buttons on his shirt—a shirt that's clinging to him like a second skin.

Solid muscle exists beneath the clothes. Muscle and hot, hard *man*.

I tear my mouth from his to see the torso I've revealed, my gaze roaming over him in open appreciation. Because *wow*. "*Why* do you wear clothes?" I demand. "*Ciprian*, you're… you're…"

"Very aroused and ready to fuck," he tells me, his tail flaring so wide inside me that I lose my balance.

And suddenly I'm in the air and against the wall again, his appendage leaving my heat.

"Open for me, pet," he says.

I part my lips, thinking he means my mouth.

However, he reaches between us and presses his cock to my entrance. "*Open*," he says, and I realize he wants my legs to spread impossibly wider.

I'm not sure I'm flexible enough for what he's saying, but I try, my thighs tensing as I do my best to spread myself as wide as I can for him.

It's only achievable because his lower half is literally holding me against the wall, imprisoning me with his massive form and strong build.

"Good little mate," he praises, his large head running through my damp center. "This is going to hurt, Viviana."

I swallow. "I know."

He nods.

Then he thrusts into me without warning, causing me to shriek in surprise and… and *pain.*

Agony rips through me, as I'm pretty sure *he* just damaged me irrevocably.

I expected a few temporary thrusts. Slow movements. Some time to adjust.

But that's just not Ciprian.

He… he's already moving.

Forcing my body to accept him. To embrace him. *To pleasure him.*

Tears escape my eyes, whimpers leaving my mouth.

He hushes me, his tongue chasing the dampness away, his growling purr vibrating against my chest. "You can take it, sweet pet," he says, his mouth brushing mine. "You were made for this. For me. *For my cock.*"

He thrusts so deeply into me that I forget how to breathe. All I can do is cling to him, my hands going to his shoulders as my nails dig into his flesh.

"*Ciprian.*" It's a curse. A whisper of torment. A… a demand for *more.*

"Mmm, you feel it now, don't you?" He begins to slow. "The way we fit together?"

I don't know about that, but his gradual pace is… it's… *it's infuriating.* "*Move.*"

"No." He slides all the way in to the hilt and stops, spearing me on his giant cock and holding me captive against the wall. "Tell me you love this, and I'll consider resuming." He brushes a tender kiss against my mouth that feels at odds with his other actions. "Clench that sweet pussy around me and *tell me you love this.*"

I want to spew hatred instead.

How dare he slam into me with such ferocity just to fucking stop!

"Keep. Going."

"Not until you tell me what I want to hear, pet," he coos. "How do I feel inside you? Is it the best cock you've ever experienced? The *only* cock you desire?"

"Ciprian…"

"*Tell me*, Viviana," he demands. "Tell me—"

"I love this!" I shout at him. "Now fucking move." I clamp down so hard on him that he actually hisses, and I consider that a sweet victory…

Until he pulls out of me entirely.

"*Ciprian*!"

He readjusts my lower half, then captures my mouth in a bruising kiss before slamming into me once more.

I scream.

I *bite*.

And blood fills my mouth from his tongue.

For a moment, he freezes.

But then he simply growls out one word: "*Drink*."

I do. I… I suck. I swallow. I accept him. I *claim* him.

I only belatedly realize that I just finalized the bond. But I'm too drunk on him to care. Too needy for more. Too lost to our blossoming connection to consider the fact that I expedited our union.

It doesn't matter.

This was inevitable.

He's my Ciprian.

My Strigoi King.

My. Mate.

Those two words are in my mind, my voice combining with his, and I'm instantaneously lost to the bliss of an orgasm that never ends.

Swirling. Mounting. *Flying*.

Our worlds join.

Our souls marrying in a way I never knew possible.

And suddenly he's growling my name while filling me with his seed.

It's a blur. It's magnetic. *It's mind-shattering.*

Because I can *feel* his pleasure. He's never experienced anything like this, not even in my mouth. And I hear him making proclamations to never let this end.

He's going to fuck me to oblivion.

For hours. Days. *Weeks.*

The inauguration will have to wait.

My king has a thousand years' worth of pent-up arousal that he needs to expend.

And I am more than ready to take it.

"Use me," I whisper. "Use me… until you're satisfied."

Another bold request. A dangerous desire.

But nothing about this relationship could be considered innocuous.

I came to Romania to hunt a Strigoi King.

Little did I realize that he was stalking me, too.

Now we're mated.

Seems like a fairy tale… come true.

CHAPTER TWENTY-TWO
CIPRIAN

I CARRY my mate to the bedchamber, our bodies still locked in an intimate embrace.

She told me to use her until I'm satisfied, and I fully intend to do just that.

But I want her in the bed.

Spread out.

Mine for the taking.

Her lips are on my neck, kissing the water droplets off my skin. We're both wet. Aroused. Utterly consumed with one another.

The mate-bond is still snapping into place, our minds melding on a wave of intoxicating sensation. I can feel every part of her, and I know she can sense me, too.

It's a beautiful union.

The perfect mating.

"You feel fucking amazing," I tell her, my voice a low rumble of sound even to my own ears. My beast is ready to be unleashed. Determined to fuck. To mark. *To claim.*

The shower was a mere introduction to the experience

to come. A way to take the edge off. To allow me a chance to learn.

Now I'm going to master the art of taking my mate.

Lifting her off my cock, I toss her onto the bed and smirk when her tits bounce.

"*Ciprian.*" My name leaves her on an adorable little snarl.

"Miss me already?" I ask, using my wings to carry me onto the bed.

She yelps as I pin her, the movement fast and clearly unexpected.

I follow it up by settling between her thighs and entering her again in a harsh thrust. "I'm going to enjoy filling you with my seed, little mate," I inform her, my lips near hers. "But first, I just want to feel more of your sweet cunt. Clench around me, Viviana. *Hold me.*"

She shudders, her hands going to my shoulders as she clings to me.

It's not what I meant.

But I enjoy the way her palms feel against my bare skin.

Which gives me an idea.

She's not fully lost to her heat yet, her mind very much alive and aware of our thriving connection.

I pull out of her again and roll us until I'm flat on my back with my wings splayed beneath me, and her petite form is straddling my hips.

"Explore me." I don't issue it as a request so much as a demand. But really, it's an invitation. One I hope she accepts.

I've waited a millennium for this experience. I want to prolong it. Bathe in it. Delay my gratification until my beast is roaring with the need to rut.

And I want her to be the one to teach me a lesson this time.

"Show me what you like, regina mea."

Her nipples tighten, her eyes gazing down at me with exquisite need. I can taste her arousal on my tongue, making my mouth salivate for more.

It takes restraint not to flip our positions again and place my mouth against her luscious pussy.

But as she shifts and takes hold of my cock, I find myself captivated and barely able to breathe. She angles me toward her slick heat and slides down, taking me to the hilt and rocking her alluring hips.

Gods. Her citrusy scent is everywhere, claiming this room just as much as she is claiming me.

"You want to ride me?" I ask, aware of the growl deepening my voice.

"No." She squeezes me with her cunt, drawing a hiss from my lips. "I'm *holding* you inside me while I *explore.* When I'm done… I'll consider riding you."

I arch a brow. "You'll consider it?"

She nods. "You gave me two commands—to hold you and to explore you. The first is done. The second is… something I intend to make last. So if you're patient, I'll reward you. If you're impatient, I suppose you'll reward us both by fucking me to oblivion. Win-win situation, I think."

Her levelheaded reply confirms she's very aware of our embrace, something that thrills me. While I can't wait for her heat to take over, I'm eager to play while she's capable of being in charge.

"Explore away, mate."

She presses her palms to my abdomen, her nails gently tracing lines across my stomach. "You're all muscle… I'm kind of mad that you hid this from me beneath your clothes for so long."

I smile. "Are you saying you want to keep me naked for a while?"

"For forever if you let me," she says, leaning down to press her tits to my chest and hug me. "I think I'll just... live like this." Her pussy spasms around me, causing me to growl a little.

"No moving? No petting?"

"Mm-hmm," she hums. "You wanted me to hold you... right?"

My grip on her hips tightens. "You're playing with me."

"Maybe." She presses a kiss to my shoulder, her hands trailing up my sides. "I think I'm just... loving you."

"Loving me?"

"Yes." She sounds a little confused, her mind telling me that she's considering the term and realizing that perhaps she does love me.

"You should. I'm your mate."

"But we just met."

"After years of stalking each other," I remind her with a growl. "We're connected for eternity, Viviana. Love is... what we are." I say it slowly because I'm attempting to puzzle her thoughts together with my own. "I think our mating redefines the meaning, or perhaps makes the word irrelevant."

"So you're saying this is more than lust?"

My growl shifts into a snarl. "Lust is something I feel, yes. But the yearning I have for you is far deeper than that term can singularly define." Though, I am aware I've used that term a few times, thinking about how many years' worth of lust I have for her to handle.

But this is more than a lifetime of desiring a mate. It's

about finally finding my other half. Completing my soul. *Officially feeling alive…*

Rather than comment all that aloud, I push the realizations into her mind, wanting her to understand. *Needing* her to comprehend that this is about so much more than pleasure for me.

She's my future.

The one I've spent several lifetimes hunting for, not just for the kingdom, but for *me*.

My soul's mate. My heart. *My Strigoi Queen.*

She shivers against me. "When I started researching you, I never expected… *this*. But I think I dreamt about it. And I know I fantasized about… something like this." Her mind tells me those fantasies involved a lot of sex. Biting. *Claiming*.

But she never anticipated the emotions thriving between us.

"Mates do more than fuck, Viviana." I take my hand away from her hip and glide it up her bare back to her nape, then slide my fingers into her hair to take hold of the damp strands. "You're mine to cherish, regina mea. Mine to spoil, too." I tug her head up and force her to meet my gaze. "And mine to love."

She crawls up my form, causing my cock to slip out to the tip, and presses her lips to mine.

My mate is giving up her world for me. But I don't hear a single ounce of regret in her mind.

"This is a lot more rewarding than delivering a dissertation," she says against my mouth. "I think I always knew my research would end this way. Or perhaps… perhaps I merely hoped it would. I don't know. I'm tired of trying to understand fate. I just want to feel, Ciprian. Make me *feel*."

My chest releases a low rumble of sound, my hands

falling away from her as I restrain my urges once more. "I thought you were going to explore me?"

She grabs my shoulders and pushes herself upright as she takes me to the hilt again. "I thought you wanted me to ride you?"

A chuckle escapes me, the sound a rarity. Yet I suspect this female is going to make me laugh… often. "I want you to teach me what you like, mate. Show me how to pleasure you."

"You've been doing a fine job without my instruction," she says, her voice turning husky with the words. "But I would love for you to sit up."

I consider her request and use my wings to propel me upward.

She jumps, then moans, the positioning driving me even deeper into her. "Hmm," I hum, taking hold of her hair again as my opposite palm goes to her lower back. I thrust up, drawing a sharp gasp from my mate's lips. "Yes, I do like this."

So I repeat it again.

And again.

Each punch of my hips making her cling to me more and more.

"Your pussy is strangling my cock, pet." I press a kiss to her throat, her pulse a throbbing enticement against my mouth. "Mmm, but I wonder what it would feel like… with a little more pressure."

Her nails dig into my shoulders as my tail glides up her thighs.

"Go up on your knees for a second," I tell her. "Let my cock slip out of you."

Her mind shifts from wanting to utter a denial to being curious about my intentions. Then she goes up on her knees like a good little mate.

I praise her with my thoughts but, out loud, say, "Stay just like this and don't move."

Her brow furrows a little, then she freezes as the tip of my tail slides through her damp folds. "I don't think I can… take… that… with your cock, Ciprian."

"You can and you will," I assure her. "And you're going to like it, too."

I drive the tip into her and swirl, saturating my tail.

Viviana screams at the sudden intrusion, but she doesn't move—just like I requested.

"You're so fucking good for me," I tell her, stroking her G-spot. "Keep obeying, pet. We're going to do… something else new."

Her shoulders seem to stiffen.

"Stay relaxed," I murmur, withdrawing my tail to guide it back. "I hear that's important."

Her mind catches up to my intentions just before I reach her second hole.

I don't give her time to process it as I prod it with my tail, testing the tightness of her opening.

"Ciprian…" Her mind tells me she's never done anything like this before, and not just with a tail.

She's a virgin here, a realization that makes me smile. "We'll experience this together, Viviana."

I push a little more, my tip folding in on itself to keep the flared head as slender as possible. The dampness of my tail makes this easier, allowing me to enter her somewhat easily.

But… "Fuck, you're tight back here, pet. It's going to take some work to prepare you for my cock."

Her eyes widen. "I don't think—"

"You'll take it," I interject. "When you're lost in your heat, you'll even *beg* for it."

Those beautiful tits of hers flush a pretty pink, making

me want to lick them. So I bend my head and do just that, biting and nibbling her breasts as my tail works its way into her.

When she starts to squirm, I slide my palm down from her lower back to swat at her firm ass. "No moving."

"You're… you're *torturing* me," she accuses, the moan underlining her words telling me it's a good kind of torture, not a bad one.

Of course, the way she's dripping between her thighs already confirmed that.

So rather than reply, I take her nipple between my teeth and *bite.*

She jolts, so I grab her hip to hold her steady, my opposite hand still in her hair, as I drink from her. *Gods, just think, in nine months, you'll have milk here, too…*

She shudders in response. *You're going to impregnate me during the heat.* It's not a question but recognition of a concept she already understands.

I am, I confirm. *We're going to make an heir.*

But we'll have a lifetime of ruling together before that heir takes over the kingdom.

Because that's how matings and royal cycles are supposed to work.

Something I make sure she knows with a few thoughts from my mind to hers.

Though, she's starting to lose herself to the sensations of my bite and the ministrations of my tail. "My needy little pet," I murmur after releasing her nipple. "Be a good mate and put my cock in your cunt again."

She doesn't fight me or question it, just does as I demand, then gasps when my tail flares a little in her ass.

"*Fuck,*" I whisper, marveling at the sensation. "I *felt* that." So I do it again. Because it makes her impossibly tighter. Adds more to the experience. Makes this…

unbelievable. "I'm going to fuck you like this from now on. Always ensuring you're so consumed by me that you can't think of anything else."

If she wants to protest, she can't, because I claim her mouth with my tongue, taking all three of her holes. Fucking her. Possessing her. *Filling her.*

My beast roars with triumph as my mate melts into me, accepting me as hers, and clamps down around me to ensure I can't leave.

Not that I would even try.

If anything, I just try to go farther into her, forcing her to take as much as she can with my tail, cock, and tongue.

All while monitoring her pleasure, ensuring she feels even better than I do. Which is a hard task to accomplish, given the euphoria warming my veins.

Every part of me is on fire for her. This isn't even the rut or the beginnings of it. It's simply… *us*.

I kiss her. Devour her. Fuck her. Fall into her. And find a new existence with her.

She's everything to me.

My mate.

My queen.

My destiny.

"Come for me," I beg her. "I need to feel this delicious body of yours detonate around me."

She trembles, her climax warming our bond until she does exactly as I implored her to do. Only it's even more intense. Even hotter. Even more cataclysmic than I could ever have imagined.

It's a roaring fury of need mingled with fate, and it drowns me in a sea of ecstasy, forcing me to explode right along with her.

We're both groaning. Growling. *Snarling*.

And then it hits… the urge to never stop. Not just out

of desire for our mating. Not just because I can't get enough. But an intrinsic need to *ravage* her.

She claws at me in earnest, feeling the same pull, her body and mouth and mind demanding more. More of everything. More of me. More of us. More of *this*.

We lose time.

Because it's irrelevant.

She's immortal now. I'm immortal. She's mine. I'm hers. All that exists is our passion. Our yearnings. *Our illicit cravings*.

My beast is in charge now, giving rein to my monstrous needs.

Fortunately for me, I have a queen. A feisty, confident, fearless female. My pet. My mate. Regina mea. *Mine.*

CHAPTER TWENTY-THREE
VIVI

Over a Week Later…

Strigoi are real. And the proof of it is growing inside me.

Not that I plan to write about it. Instead, I simply marvel at the development as I stare at my reflection in the bathroom mirror.

I can't see anything yet. Can't even feel it. But Ciprian woke me this morning with his tongue between my thighs, then informed me that my heat was successful.

The actions of the last eight days or so are foggy in my head. Like a really good dream that I only remember pieces of. Everything after him taking me with his tail and his cock is a blur. Yet I know we did… *a lot.*

Biting.

Penetrating in all ways.

So much licking.

Sucking.

Swallowing.

My cheeks heat with that last one since I can still taste

Ciprian in my mouth. But that part I remember every moment of since it just happened in the shower.

He walks out behind me, his expression one of satisfaction as he takes in the mirror before us. "You're beautiful, regina mea." He places a kiss against my throat, his eyes holding mine in the reflection. "Thank you for being mine."

I smile. "Is this the part where we talk about how I never had a choice?"

He frowns. "Viviana—"

I turn in his arms and press my palm to his cheek. "I've been obsessed with you for years, Ciprian. You captured my heart in that illustration, and it's been yours ever since. This… this is where I'm meant to be. Choice or no."

Because I don't mean that he took me against my will, just that fate entangled me in a web I could never leave.

"You'll always have a choice with me," he replies, cupping my cheek as well. "That's why you have a safe word, yes?"

My lips curl again. "I'm pretty sure I'm never going to use it."

"That's good," he replies. "Because I don't think our Strigoi will like hearing their queen talk about *vampires*."

I nod sagely. "Yes, I can see why they might be jealous."

His eyes narrow. "There is *nothing* to be jealous about. Strigoi can fly. We also have tails." He wraps his around my calf and slides it upward between my thighs. "We are quite superior, regina mea."

"I would ask for a demonstration of that superiority, but you just gave me one."

"Perhaps you need another?" he offers. "I'm more than happy to…" He trails off, his pointed ears seeming to twitch as he slowly looks at the bathroom door. "We have visitors."

My brow furrows. "Visitors?"

He nods, not looking pleased. "Come." He grabs a towel and pulls me into the walk-in closet off the bathroom.

Goose bumps pebble all over my sensitive skin as he dries me with the soft cotton, his movements gentle yet thorough.

When he selects a dark red dress for me to wear, I stare at it. "Who does this belong to?"

"You." He starts assembling a suit—which has a similar shirt to match the gown.

"But the Strigoi didn't know my size or anything about me until last week."

"Not true," he murmurs. "They knew a great deal about you. But the clothes arrived yesterday. I put them away while you slept."

I blink at him, then scan over the long row of items taking up an entire wall. "All of these came in yesterday?"

"Yes." He glances at me. "What troubles you, pet?"

"I… I just assumed…" I trail off, studying him and then the items again. As well as a dresser in the middle.

Without asking, I go and open a drawer to find lingerie tucked inside.

Lingerie that reminds me of my time in Negru Castle.

It's the same French brand.

"Are these from my old room?" I ask him.

"Yes. You never had a chance to wear them, so I brought them here."

"And they weren't from an old mistress," I say, more to myself than to him. Because I know he never really had one of those.

However, he responds with, "I bought them for your

visit, as I fully expected to make you walk around in my castle in nothing but gowns or silky panties. But my plans were derailed. So we'll just… make it a rule for here instead."

"A rule?" I echo, facing him again, my eyebrow rising. "What kind of *rule*?"

"One where you are required to only wear items from that dresser when in our rooms. Or you can choose to be naked." He smiles then as he adds, "You do like choices, right?"

"A somewhat joke from the usually serious Strigoi King?" I say, feigning shock. "Are you feeling all right?" I take a step forward and try to touch his forehead, but he grabs my wrist before I can complete the action and tugs me into a kiss.

Warmth reignites in my lower belly, my body instantly on fire for him as he parts my lips to dominate me with his tongue. But just as quickly as it began, it stops, his hand in my hair yanking me back to stare up at him. "I'm only this way with you," he tells me. "Remember that. It's going to be important soon."

I arch a brow. "You're telling me I'm the only one you can be funny around?"

"You're the only one who will ever see me smile," he corrects me, his teeth nipping my lower lip. "Now get dressed, mate. I want to see that red gown on you so I can fantasize about removing it later."

"Seems like a waste," I say as he releases me. "Just keep me naked."

"If Marius wasn't waiting in my sitting room, I would consider that." His eyes roam over my breasts before returning to my face. "Stop stalling and put on the dress."

"I'm not stalling, just talking." I proceed to prove my point by donning the red silk fabric. It looks a bit formal with my wet hair, but I don't really care. "Happy?" I ask after he turns to face me in his perfectly pressed suit.

"Am I happy that you chose not to wear anything underneath that sexy dress?" he returns. "Yes and no."

I huff a laugh. "I seem to recall you being quite upset with me during our first dinner together—for wearing underwear."

"I was *disappointed*, not *upset*. And that was only because I wanted you to wear the lingerie I'd purchased for you." He cants his head. "I spent a great deal of time researching items specifically with you in mind. I very much want to see you model them for me."

"Maybe I'll do that after Marius leaves," I suggest.

"Oh, I hope you do," he replies, sauntering toward me and leaning in to give me a kiss. "But I suspect you'll be busy."

"Busy?" I echo, curious as to what kinky activity he has in mind.

He grabs my hand and leads me into the bathroom. "Yes."

"Doing what?" I prod, wanting to know more.

"Talking, probably," he replies.

My brow furrows. "What?" *Does he mean like… dirty talk?* I wonder, confused.

No. Absolutely not, he replies into my mind. *I'm a possessive Strigoi, regina mea. The only one you will speak to in that manner is me.* He pauses at the threshold between the bathroom and the bedroom.

"You are *mine*," he adds out loud in a lethally quiet voice. "I do not share."

I swallow. "I don't share either."

"Good."

"Good," I repeat.

His lips twitch again. "You're the perfect queen."

"I haven't been crowned yet," I remind him as we exit the bathroom.

"You're my queen regardless of a crown," he replies, his tone flatter than before.

And I realize why as we near the sitting room. *Marius*. Ciprian mentioned he was here, which means he's putting on the stoic façade for his best friend.

Why don't you let him see you smile? I wonder at my mate through our mental link.

Because he would tease me relentlessly for it, Ciprian replies into my head. *I've often remarked that he smiles too much.*

Why?

Because he fucking smiles too much, Ciprian mutters. *Though, he doesn't appear to be all that amused right now…*

That last comment ironically comes through with a hint of amusement in Ciprian's mental voice, making me curious about what he seems to know.

But before I can ask, Marius's voice sounds from the seating area. "Thank fuck. Can you please present your mate and free me of this nonsense?"

"By 'nonsense,' you mean the loose ends you were supposed to take care of?" Ciprian replies at the same time a familiar voice begins to demand, "Who are…? Oh."

"Yes, if you would allow others to speak rather than assuming you're the center of all attention, you may learn some things," Marius deadpans.

"*Gaby*?" I attempt to sprint around the corner, to see into the seating area, but Ciprian's hand in mine yanks me back since his big body doesn't move as fast.

"Vivi?" my best friend asks.

"There. Proof of life. Am I excused?" The irritation in Marius's voice is very unlike the playful tones he used with me.

"No." Ciprian's word echoes through the room, preceding our entry into the seating area.

Gaby jumps up and runs for me.

I try to meet her halfway, but Ciprian doesn't release my hand, causing me to embrace my best friend in an awkward one-arm hug.

"Thank God you're okay," Gaby breathes, ignoring the hulking Strigoi King beside us. "When that damn vampire came to use his voodoo on me, I suspected the worst."

"Problems with your compulsion?" The silky quality of Ciprian's question has Marius issuing a grunt from the other side of the room.

"Seems this one is somehow immune to my charms," Marius mutters.

"Charms." Gaby snorts and releases me to round on Marius. "*You* are a barbarian."

"I'm not."

"You *are*. You threw me over your shoulder and whisked me off to this realm without so much as an invitation or even a kiss. I expected wooing. Maybe the best fuck of my life. But this? *This* is not how the books go."

"You and your prattling on about *books*," Marius hisses, coming to his feet and advancing on Gaby.

My eyes widen, my instinct to get between them thwarted by my mate holding me back. *Ciprian!*

Shh, he hushes into my mind. *I'm rather enjoying this. Please let it continue.*

He's going to hurt my friend, I snap back at him, trying to free my hand so I can reach Gaby.

Actually, I rather think she might hurt him, he murmurs, his grip easily holding me back.

"You could learn something from those stories," she tells him, her finger colliding with his chest.

"I don't need to *read* to know how to properly take care

of a human, little nuisance," he snarls back at her. "I have an entire harem you can interview on the topic."

Gaby scoffs at that. "Like I'm interested in hearing about your sex life."

"Yet you continue to talk about me fucking you."

"No, I continue talking about how you've ruined my expectations of meeting a vampire—"

"*Strigoi*," he growls.

But she acts as though she hasn't heard him and presses onward. "You're supposed to seduce me, bite me, and make me scream in a good way. Not kidnap me and hold me in a cage!"

"My bedchamber is *not* a cage."

"It is when I don't wish to be there."

"And whose fault is that?" he demands, folding his arms.

"The asshole who put me there?" she suggests.

"You're forgetting why that happened, little nuisance," he returns. "You were in a guest suite before that, and you—"

"Tried to *explore*," she says, finishing the statement for him.

"You tried to *escape*," he corrects her. "Thus requiring me to lock you in my room to babysit." He finally looks away from her and at Ciprian. "Can you please take over now?"

"No." That seems to be Ciprian's favorite word of the day where his best friend is concerned. "This is your mess. Fix it."

Marius looks offended. "How is this *my* mess? *You* chose a human mate from another realm, and I had to go make sure no one notices her absence. I dealt with her parents, I—"

"My parents?" I interrupt, my stomach twisting. "What did you do to my parents, Marius?"

Not that I… that I have a lot of contact with them. They were always much more interested in themselves than in my life. They didn't even know what I was studying at the university since I was paying for it all on my own with scholarships.

"I informed them that you accepted an internship in Romania and would be relocating there permanently. You'll need to visit every now and then to make it believable, but my compulsion helped pave the way," Marius says. "Not that they were hard to compel. Unlike *this* devious thing."

"Devious thing." Gaby turns around to look at me. "You couldn't have found a sexier vampire to send me? Really?"

"Now you're insulting my physical appearance?" I was wrong before. Marius didn't look offended after Ciprian's commentary. Because this is what he looks like when offended. "I'm the sexiest *Strigoi* you'll ever meet."

Gaby huffs a humorless laugh. "I'm currently looking at a much hotter Strigoi, so I doubt that very much." Her eyes travel over Ciprian as she speaks, causing me to frown.

I move in front of Ciprian—an action he allows—and step backward into him. "This one is *mine*."

He chuckles into my head, though I don't feel him express it aloud. However, his arms come around me, and he presses a kiss to my temple. "Very much yours, regina mea," he murmurs, the words warming my heart.

"Doesn't detract from the point that Marius is clearly lying about being the *sexiest Strigoi* I'll ever meet." She faces the male in question again. "You are insufferable."

"Pot, meet pot."

"It's 'pot, meet kettle,' moron."

"Whatever," he growls. "Your *humanisms* are beneath me."

"Yeah, well, your *vampirisms* are beneath *me*," she retorts, the pair of them staring each other down.

My brow furrows, and I rotate in Ciprian's arms to face him. *What other loose ends did he handle?* I ask via our mental bond.

I'm not entirely sure, but I assume your university links and all traces of your research have likely disappeared. He studies me. *Does that bother you?*

I consider it for a long moment, then slowly shake my head. *I don't need all of that when I have you.*

It's the utmost truth.

Everything I did was in an effort to find him. To prove he existed. And it was never really about sharing that proof with the world so much as with myself. I needed to know that he was real. That was always for me… not the university.

And we'll visit my parents at some point? I ask, frowning a little. *I doubt they'll miss me much.* As it is, I haven't seen them in about six months.

To keep up appearances, yes. But at some point, we will either have to disappear entirely or use compulsion to help alter their memories.

My frown deepens. *You don't want them to be able to identify you?*

I don't want them to notice you've stopped aging, he corrects me.

Oh. My nose crinkles. *Yeah, that makes sense.* I hadn't really thought about that aspect of everything. *What about…?* I press my palm to my belly. *Will we visit with our baby?* I'm not sure that would be safe for our child. But I also don't know how I feel about our baby not knowing my family at all.

We can make arrangements, regina mea. I originally thought you may never see your home world again, but I think we can find ways to go back and forth as needed. However, most of our time will need to be here—in the Strigoi Kingdom.

I nod. *I think that's safest.* I don't want to risk anyone in my home realm finding out about me or Ciprian or our child. *It would be unfortunate if someone took a photo of us for others to find in the future.*

Or perhaps a stroke of fate, he returns. *That illustration is how you discovered my existence, after all.*

I don't want anyone else to know about you. You're mine.

Yes, I believe we've established that, Viviana, he says, his amusement palpable via our bond even though his face remains stoic. *Don't worry, pet. I'm just as possessive of you.* He leans down to brush his nose against mine. *Now, I think it may be wise for you to rein in your friend before she murders mine.*

I blink, then look back at Gaby to find her hands fisted at her sides. I'm not sure what she and Marius have been saying to each other, but Ciprian is right—she looks ready to strangle someone.

"If I had a stake, I would drive it into your heart!" she shouts.

Marius smirks. "All that would do is piss me off more, sweetheart. And you're doing a fine job of that without the violence."

Gaby releases a growl and spins toward me. "How do I kill him?"

"I don't know," I admit, my brow coming down. *How do you kill a Strigoi?* I mentally ask my mate.

For research purposes or pleasurable ones? he wonders.

For curiosity's sake, I reply.

Destruction of the mind, typically by beheading and setting the remains on fire, he informs me, his blunt words causing me to blink.

"I, uh, I don't think killing is a good idea," I say, the words for Gaby. "Marius is Ciprian's best friend, and he helped me find Negru Castle." It sounds lame to my ears, and clearly registers that way for Gaby, too.

"Seriously?" She gapes at me. "*Seriously?*"

"See? Other people like me," Marius boasts.

"Well, I didn't say that," I insert.

But he's not paying any attention to me now. He's entirely focused on my simmering best friend. Her dark curls bounce as she turns around to glare at him again. "You've clearly compelled her."

He tilts his head back and looks at the ceiling above with a groan. "My Gods, female, you are *infuriating.*"

I think we should let them keep flirting, Ciprian murmurs into my mind. *Meanwhile, we'll go get some breakfast. You and the baby need food.*

I don't know if this is flirting. My brow crinkles again. *But… but food is probably good. So long as you're sure Marius won't throttle my friend.*

Hmm, I can't promise that. Something tells me your best friend may enjoy some strangulation.

I blanch at that. *What?*

But I am certain Marius won't hurt her in a way she dislikes, Ciprian goes on. *Her being here means she's our guest, and given her relationship with you, she's very much under my protection. Marius knows better than to disrespect me in that way.*

"We are going to breakfast," Ciprian announces before I can reply. "Please continue to entertain our guest, Marius." He folds his wings around me, confusing me a little about his intentions, as it's going to make walking difficult.

"You cannot be—"

The words are cut off by the room vanishing around

us. Not that I could see much beyond Ciprian's wings, but the ceiling disappears.

Only for a dark sky to appear in a blink.

His gray wings unfold, allowing me to see that we're now in a courtyard. Or rather, a garden full of exquisite black roses.

I stare at the gorgeous landscaping, then glance up at the blood moons above in the obsidian sky, then back at the enchanted flowers. There's a blanket with a basket waiting for us in what appears to be silver-like grass.

"What is this?" I ask, distracted from the conversation we just left. "And you can *teleport*? Or do you have a portal thingy?"

This time, he allows me to hear the chuckle from his lips, confirming we're alone out here. "Ah, regina mea, there is so much I need to teach you about the Strigoi." He presses his lips to my throat. "I requested a picnic before our shower. The basket is empty, but it can create whatever you desire."

"Like the refrigerator your father used?"

"Yes, just like that," he murmurs.

"Oh." I swallow, suddenly parched. And hungry. And… and *enamored*.

"Also, yes, I can teleport. But only a few miles in distance. I think the *portal thingy*, which is called a *portal key*, is still with my father."

My head spins. One would think by now I would be used to all the otherworldly magic and Ciprian's abilities. But I suspect it'll take years for me to become accustomed to everything.

As he said, there's still a lot for him to teach me.

"I guess you could give me a lesson now," I say, my hands going to his chest to begin sliding upward. "But I have a request."

One of his dark brows wings upward. "Oh?" His hands grasp my hips as he pulls me closer to him. "Name it."

"I would like to sit in your lap while I eat." I pitch my voice low. "And I expect your tail to provide encouragement while I learn."

Crimson bleeds into his dark eyes, causing my stomach to ignite with butterflies. "I think I can accommodate that *request*," he murmurs, his tail already sneaking up my leg. "Let's eat, Viviana."

"Yes, my king… let's *eat*." My arms slip around his neck as I go up onto my toes to get even closer to him. "Although, what you'll be eating can't be found in that basket, Ciprian." My words are a whisper against his lips. "Because you'll be dining between my thighs for breakfast."

"Then I expect you to drink from my cock," he returns without missing a beat.

"Sounds like an excellent meal," I tease.

Not sure it's the most nutritious of ventures, but I don't voice that part aloud.

I simply give in to the urge to kiss him.

And sigh into his embrace.

No more dissertations.

No more proposed theories.

This is simply my reality now.

Because Strigoi are real… and I mated the Strigoi King.

EPILOGUE

CIPRIAN

Two Years Later

"Careful, cara mea," I murmur as a little bundle of darkness attempts to fly across the courtyard. "Your wings are not ready for that yet."

My daughter doesn't listen, too excited by the fluttering at her back to hear me or anyone else.

When she topples over, I jump forward to help her. But she just gets back up and tries again. There's no question in my mind about where her tenacity comes from. And I allow that thought to flow to my mate as she eats a grilled cheese on a blanket nearby.

I still haven't tried it, despite her constantly asking me to take a bite. It's a game between us now, one I refuse to lose.

Emilia's tenacity comes from you, too, my king, Viviana replies.

Out loud, she says, "We're planning a visit next month." Her words are for Gaby, as she just asked if we had any intentions of venturing into the human realm.

"We can't take Emilia, though. Her wings are like her father's and don't vanish. While Ciprian could use compulsion to hide her Strigoi traits—like he does for himself—we can't risk her safety."

"Ah, so she inherited her mother's beauty and her father's weaker traits," Marius muses, looking at me. "Seems par for the course where your shortcomings are concerned, hmm?"

I narrow my gaze. "Our daughter has superior traits from both her parents, marking her as perfect in every way."

He smirks. "If you say so."

"Just because your wings are inferior to mine does not mean you can insult my daughter," I growl at him.

Amusement brightens his gaze. "Was that an invitation to spar, Cip? Because that's how I interpreted it."

I sigh and shake my head. "I should never have let you stay here." He owns one of the wings of my palace—a gift I gave him for serving as temporary king in my absence.

Alas, most days, I regret that decision.

Although, having Gaby nearby makes my mate happy. Which helps cool my annoyance at Marius's constant appearances throughout my day.

He and Gaby finally mated about three months ago, the evidence of which is currently growing inside the female.

Viviana was thrilled.

I was merely… amused.

Gaby certainly made her mate work for her affection, something I enjoyed observing.

But right now, I very much want to take my best friend up on his offer to spar. If nothing more than to have an excuse to punch him in his grinning face.

He still smiles far too much.

Though, in secret, I think I may smile even more.

Because my mate and our child have brought me immense joy.

They've settled my soul. Created a new era for the Strigoi Kingdom. And taught me how to love in a way I never knew imaginable.

A love that only deepens now as my daughter attempts to fly into my arms. "*Up*," she commands, causing my lips to twist in a ghost of a smile.

"Having a seizure over there?" Marius asks.

I ignore him and lift my daughter into my arms instead. I'll take him up on his sparring when I return.

Because *up* means Emilia wants to fly. And just like her mother, I'm a slave to her wishes. I'll give both of them everything I am. For eternity.

I'm theirs in a way I'll never belong to anyone else.

"Want to join us, mate?" I ask Viviana as I situate Emilia on one hip.

Viviana practically jumps off the blanket to run for me—very much like our daughter just did—causing me to grin in full.

Marius comments something else that I ignore, my focus entirely on my family.

They're my life now. My world. My reason for existing.

It's strange to think that I lived over a thousand years without them. It's like I was barely alive then. Now, I'm truly breathing. Truly existing. *Truly reigning.*

"Let's fly," I say, embracing my mate and our daughter, then flap my wings to take us to the sky.

Emilia squeals with delight.

While Viviana simply sighs with contentment, her mind completely at ease.

I love you, my fearless queen, I whisper into her thoughts.

I love you, too, she whispers back. *My Strigoi King…*

USA Today Bestselling Author Lexi C. Foss loves to play in dark worlds, especially the ones that bite. She lives in North Carolina with her family. When not writing, she's busy crossing items off her travel bucket list, or chasing eclipses around the globe. She's quirky, consumes way too much coffee, and loves to swim.

Want access to the most up-to-date information for all of Lexi's books? Sign-up for her newsletter here.

Lexi also likes to hang out with readers on Facebook in her exclusive readers group - Join Here.

Where To Find Lexi:
www.LexiCFoss.com

www.ingramcontent.com/pod-product-compliance
Lightning Source LLC
LaVergne TN
LVHW091035080826
845145LV00002B/500